WINDOWS OF LOVE

CAROL MONCADO

Cover photos: Copyright:
Couple: TijanaM/depositphotos.com
Snowman Window: Mandy Grant, Grants Goods
Town: Stewart Johnson
Author photo: Captivating by Keli, 2010
First edition, CANDID Publications, 2020

CHAPTER 1

DECEMBER 13, 2020

Small towns held great appeal.

Or so Dean Krazowski had always been told.

He didn't get it.

He couldn't order Chinese food at midnight if he wanted to. He couldn't even get Chinese food in this town.

Not that he ever ordered Chinese food unless a client wanted some.

But that wasn't the point.

He walked the streets of Trumanville, Missouri and wondered what on earth had possessed him to come to a town with less people than his block in New York.

Shoving his hands into the pockets of his jacket, he wondered where he *could* eat in a town this size. There was a bakery across the street from where he walked. He stopped and debated jaywalking.

A shove at his back made him stumble into the street.

"Oh, my goodness! I'm so sorry." The female voice must accompany the hands that grabbed his arm and pulled him back onto the sidewalk.

Neither one of those things would happen in Manhattan.

Well, being pushed into the street might, but not by a door opening. The sidewalks were too wide in most places.

"Are you all right?"

Dean finally looked at the young woman, juggling an armload of canvases and a tote bag, and smiled. "I'm fine. Thank you."

"I'm so sorry. I'm going to be late for my class, and I didn't look to see if anyone was outside when I came out."

He glanced at the building. The storefront had to be well over a hundred years old, but rather than windows full of questionable antiques, they were covered by curtains.

"I'm fine." He made a shooing motion with his hand. "Go on."

"Thank you." She hurried off, calling "I'm sorry" behind her as she did.

Dean thought about laughing but sighed instead. A message came in on his watch. His suite still wasn't ready and wouldn't be any time soon. He reserved a very specific suite at the resort on the southern shore of Serenity Lake.

But it wasn't ready, and they didn't know when it would be. With a growl under his breath, Dean started for the diner down the street. He could at least get something hot to eat.

Three people entered the building before him. The number of cars outside concerned him a little. But surely there weren't enough people in a town this size who ate at the diner rather than at home. Sit down, Sunday night dinners were still a thing in the Midwest, weren't they?

His hopes dropped as he walked in. Every table was full and so were the bar stools.

A waitress walked by with a coffee pot in her hand. "If you want to wait, you're welcome to, but you're probably lookin' at about half an hour, sugar. If you want something to take with you, let me know." Then she winked at him. "If you want a new adoptive grandma, Mrs. Braverman will take you in. Last booth on your right. She'll even treat ya."

The bill didn't concern him at all. Dean looked to his right to find an older woman seated against the wall. She waved him over.

Well, he'd be sitting farther away from her than if he was on the subway. His stomach rumbled in confirmation that this was his best choice.

He slid into the other side of the booth, uncomfortable with keeping his back to the door, but having little choice. He held out a hand. "Hello. I'm Dean. You must be Mrs. Braverman."

She shook his hand. "I am. Thank you for joining me. Mr. Braverman has the flu. I'm avoiding him like the plague so I don't get it."

Dean nodded. "Makes sense." He glanced around. "Is it always this busy?"

Mrs. Braverman laughed. "Heavens no, though this is the best place to get a stick-to-your-ribs meal. Every family in here has someone at home who's sick, and they're all trying to stay healthy. The flu has run rampant through our little town. The school even closed a week early for Christmas break."

He thanked the waitress for his water and the menu, but frowned as he thought about the illness sweeping the town. "Did no one get a flu shot?"

Another laugh. "Oh, yes. But we've got a different strain running through here. It'll all blow over by Christmas, but until then, some of us are kind of staying away to keep ourselves healthy."

"Does Mr. Braverman need help? Is he all right at home by himself?"

Mrs. Braverman waved a hand. "He's fine. He's sleeping and hasn't been eating much anyway. I'll take him some soup home. You're an out-of-towner. Staying at the resort, the B&B, or a KrazBnB?"

He hadn't even considered staying at a KrazBnB. Why not? He owned the company, but it hadn't even occurred to him that there might be a place he'd be willing to stay in this area. "I have reservations at the resort, but I reserved a specific room, and it's not ready. They can't tell me when it will be."

"Why not take a different room?"

He looked over the menu, considering that. "I wanted that particular room for a reason."

"Then go somewhere else. There's a lovely KrazBnB a block or so from here. It's an 1880s storefront converted into a couple of apartments and three KrazBnBs."

"I hadn't thought about it," he told her honestly.

"I'm sure the Milligan girls have at least one of the spaces open," Mrs. Braverman went on. "They took it over from their grandparents." She leaned closer. "They've both had this flu going around. The older of the two girls has been helping take care of their grandparents while they recover. The younger one is running the KrazBnB while substitute teaching and art lessons and those group painting classes where everyone makes the same picture."

Classes? Wasn't the woman who'd run into him on her way to give some classes?

He pulled out his phone and opened the correct app. Sure enough, there were two available KrazBnBs very close to him. After looking at the photos, he chose the larger of the two and reserved it. He might as well try out his own app and see how it worked. It had been a long time since he'd done so. His security team would likely have a fit, but they already weren't happy that he was here without them.

"Thank you for the recommendation," he told Mrs. Braverman as he took another glance at the menu. "I appreciate it."

The waitress came by again to take his order. The next couple of weeks had the potential to be much better than he expected - or much worse.

WENDY MILLIGAN JUGGLED her bag with her art supplies, four canvases, and a large soda as she tried to dig her phone out of her pocket.

That particular buzzing pattern meant one of the KrazBnBs had a message or rental.

She groaned when she saw the message on the screen. It was good that the larger of the rentals was reserved, but technically check-in could begin any time after three in the afternoon, and it was already much later than that.

It was clean. That was taken care of already, but when she hadn't had a reservation come in, she hadn't pulled out any of the Christmas decorations.

She'd been just too busy.

The last couple of weeks she'd been substitute teaching every day, painting windows in the evenings or on weekends, and running everything else while her sister took care of their grandparents, who were both down with the flu. Normally, they both did more in a day than Wendy preferred to do in a week, but this virus hit them both hard.

There simply hadn't been time to decorate when the units were vacant.

Once inside the community center where her Painting with Pals class would be held, she dumped everything on the table. Praying it would be one of her usuals who wouldn't care about the decorations, she opened the app.

And frowned.

Normally, it gave her the full name of the person who made the reservation, but this time it only gave her a username. Great. That meant it was a VIP. Very few people were granted the use of only a username. The person had great ratings, though, and lots of them.

It made her feel even worse that it wasn't decorated. If it was some VIP, then the person likely had enough clout to get ahold of Kraz himself to complain.

Could her sister get over and at least put some garland on the banister?

No. She hadn't been sleeping much, between taking care of Nana and Papa, cleaning of the units, working part-time at the bakery, and helping Wendy with their side-hustles.

Not that Wendy had slept much either.

With a sigh, she tapped out a quick personalized message then copied and pasted her standard instructions into the box. It had the key code as well as her YadaYada voice-over-internet-protocol number so she'd get messages on her phone but not give out her actual number.

She set up the community center for her painting class. Usually, the once-a-week class was full with locals and visitors alike. This week, she'd nearly canceled, but the two people still scheduled to come had pleaded with her via text to keep the class.

Mama Beach and her niece, Lani, walked in together as she finished getting everything ready.

"Thank you, Wendy," Mama Beach called as she took her coat off and tossed it on one of the extra tables. "I know you'd rather be home getting some rest, but we appreciate you being here."

"Harrison and I are supposed to make the presents this year," Lani told her. "I just wish that I could be there to watch him make one for me. Royal boy isn't exactly the most creative. I'd wait for another day, but we leave for San Majoria in the morning. His sister, Jacqueline Grace, is finally getting married."

Though several royal families had ties to the Serenity Landing area, Lani marrying Prince Harrison of San Majoria was pretty much the biggest thing to ever happen in Trumanville - except for the HEA TV movie that premiered the night before. Attending that event was the biggest thing that had happened in Wendy's life so far.

The door banged open to let someone else in. Wendy looked up to see Jazz Jackson rush in.

"Please tell me you have room for one more?" Jazz clasped her hands together as she pleaded.

Wendy smiled outwardly, but inside she cringed a bit. She loved Jazz, everyone did, but the woman could be a lot. The extrovert's extrovert with a bit of a wild streak - at least what passed for a wild streak in conservative Trumanville. The studded nose ring and blue-green hair probably made her parents roll their eyes - but if that was the worst thing she did, it would all be fine.

If Wendy could survive her chatter.

"Of course," Wendy told her. "Have a seat."

"Yay! What are we painting?" Jazz sat down on the other side of Mama Beach.

"A snowman," Wendy told her. "Nothing too exciting." Nothing she would have thought Jazz would like - way too plain for the vivacious young woman.

"Fantastic!"

For the next hour, they went through the process to make a snowman in the middle of an evergreen forest.

As expected, Jazz kept up a steady stream of conversation. Mama Beach and Lani were both content to let her, though they joined in whole-heartedly.

When they were finished, all three of them took turns blow drying their canvases so they wouldn't get any paint in their cars.

Jazz was still chattering with them when they left.

Mama Beach came back in as Wendy cleaned up. "I love that girl, but she can talk." She gave a slight shake of her head. "Sometimes quiet can be good."

"Agreed." Wendy picked up her example canvas and the one she'd made as the others worked.

"What can I take?"

Wendy shook her head. "I've got this. Could you lock up behind me?"

"Of course."

A blast of cold air hit Wendy as she walked out of the building.

Her apartment, in the same building as the KrazBnBs, was only about a block away, but walking it would take what was left of her energy.

"Goodnight, Mama Beach," she called over her shoulder as the older woman locked the door and stuck her keys back in her pockets.

She reached the front door to her apartment and dug the keys out.

"Hey."

Wendy turned to look toward the door to the largest of the units. She pasted on her widest smile. "Hi! You must be Kraz-User01. Welcome to Trumanville."

He frowned. "I am, but I have a problem. Is this your rental?"

Good thing the smile was glued in place. "It is. Let me set my things down inside, and I'll be right back to help you."

He gave a single nod.

Once in the door, her smile slipped as she dropped the things on the table. She blinked the tears of stress back and slipped the smile back in place as she headed out the door to face this guy.

If only it didn't feel like she was headed for her doom.

CHAPTER 2

W as that the same woman who'd run into him earlier in the day? Dean suspected it was, though he hadn't gotten a very good look at her either time.

A minute after she entered the other door, the woman came back out.

She gave him a big smile, though it didn't quite reach her eyes. She held out a gloved hand. "Hi. I'm Wendy."

He shook her hand, uncertain of what to make of the spark he felt. That was new. "Dean."

"Hi, Dean. What can I help you with?"

Opening the door to the cozy living area, he waited to let her in first. Normally, he was careful about being alone with a woman - he'd seen one too many friends falsely accused of something in the hopes of a payout - but Wendy put him at ease for reasons he didn't understand.

"I'm trying to get some work done, but the internet speeds aren't what I need." He pointed to his laptop sitting on the coffee table.

Her brows pulled together. "That's odd. I haven't heard anything about service issues."

"It's working," he told her. "Just not very fast."

"Hm." She picked up the remote and turned on the television. With a few clicks, she had MyBingeFlix pulled up and clicked on some reality show about a baseball player and his wife holed up in a house somewhere.

After buffering for what seemed like an eternity but was probably only ten or fifteen seconds, it began to stream. "It looks like it's working right," she told him. "Sometimes it slows down and you can't stream, but it looks to be working just fine."

Dean tried not to frown. "This is as fast as it gets?"

"I guess? I've never tested speeds or whatever unless I'm having issues and they tell me to on the phone." She stopped the episode as drone footage of the courthouse up the street caught his eye. This show was local?

He stifled a sigh. "You're telling me this is as fast as it gets?"

"I guess? Most people want to be able to stream television. As long as that works, they're fine. I'm pretty sure we have the top tier though." She shrugged. "It's small-town Midwest. It's what we have."

It wasn't really her fault, he supposed, so he turned his attention to the other thing that had been bothering him. "I am curious why the photos show Christmas decorations but there aren't any."

Her shoulders slumped downward then she straightened, fire flashing from her eyes. "I haven't had time. My sister and I run these units for our grandparents. They've both been sick with this flu that's going around. She's taking care of them, working part-time at the bakery, and helping with my side hustle."

She took a deep breath but went on before he could say anything. "I'm a substitute teacher. I teach painting classes some evenings. I draw on chalkboard menus and signs. I paint windows for businesses. I've had someone staying in this unit and the others virtually non-stop. The only days it's been unoccupied, I've had a thousand other things going on. I was going to decorate tomorrow, because it was vacant and the school is shut down for the rest of the week because so many people have been sick. That's why it's not decorated."

Dean inclined his head. "I understand." He didn't really. She couldn't hire someone to help?

"If you'll be gone for a while tomorrow, I'll come in and decorate then, if that's all right with you," she went on. "I'm happy to."

He shook his head. "I have a meeting with an employee tomorrow, but he's a local who is coming here."

"Oh. Well, if you're out of the building for a few hours, let me know, and I'll get a tree and at least some of the decorations up."

He could hear exhaustion in her voice and see it written all over her face. "Listen, I'll be done with my meeting by noon or so. If you'd like, I'll help you with the decorating. It's been a long time since I helped decorate a tree."

Dean had people for that now.

He came home one day and the house was decorated. He hadn't spent much time thinking about it - and the themes were different every year.

"You would do that?" Was that a wave of relief crossing her face?

"I would." He glanced at the ceilings that had to be at least fifteen feet tall. "Besides, if you're hanging anything, you shouldn't be on a ladder by yourself."

She grimaced. "Good point. I have a friend who missed the last step on the ladder coming out of a barn loft last summer. It took her months to get back to normal. She basically couldn't get out of bed for weeks because she had huge bruises deep inside and tore some of the muscles around her rib cage."

He winced with her. "That sounds awful. Please don't get on a ladder without someone here - me or someone else."

Wendy nodded at him. "I won't."

"Good." He tilted his head toward his laptop. "I don't mean to be rude, but I do need to get back to work, especially if the speeds aren't going to be what I'm used to."

She started for the door. "I'm sorry we don't have the speeds you're used to. Maybe once that new satellite thing is up and running, we'll be able to get faster internet here in the middle of nowhere." Her smile said she hadn't taken it too seriously. There was nothing she could do about it if she already offered the best internet available.

"I've heard great things about it," he told her. He didn't tell her he was part of the group funding it.

Wendy opened the door. "I'm sorry we don't have what you're used to, but I'm glad you're here. I hope you enjoy your stay in Trumanville."

"Thank you. I'm sure I will."

This time the smile reached her beautiful blue eyes. "And thank you for the offer to help. Shoot me a text when you're ready. I should be home working all morning."

Dean smiled back. Could he find a way to have lunch with her before decorating?

The door closed behind her. When had he decided it was time to be interested in a woman again?

RATHER THAN WORKING ALL MORNING, Wendy found herself up all night, working on gift tags for the booth at the Christmas festival until nearly four.

Then she slept through her alarm and didn't wake up until nearly noon.

Bolting out of bed when she saw the time on her phone, Wendy practically ran to the kitchen. The coffee her sister left for her had turned to sludge. Groaning, she hoped she'd have time to stop by the bakery to get one before Dean texted.

After a quick shower, she stared at her closet. She needed to wear something cute. Because he was cute.

And she'd felt something when they shook hands the night before.

A pair of skinny jeans would be good. And layers. It would be cold outside, but once they started decorating the inside of the unit, she wouldn't want a bulky sweater.

She put on a long-sleeved thermal shirt and stuck her thumbs through the holes near the cuffs. After that came a Trumanville Tigers t-shirt then a hoodie from her college years.

Comfortable really was more important than cute, right? Especially if she was going to be decorating a twelve-foot Christmas tree and hanging decorations all over the loft.

Before she could leave a text came in.

I'M READY WHEN YOU ARE. I ORDERED WAY TOO MUCH FOR LUNCH. IF YOU HAVEN'T EATEN, WOULD YOU CARE TO JOIN ME?

It relieved Wendy. She texted back. IF YOU HAVE COFFEE... I'M SOLD.

He sent back a laughing emoji and said he'd put on a fresh pot.

Not wanting to seem too eager, Wendy forced herself to move slowly as she put on her shoes and socks then grabbed her jacket and keys. She wouldn't need the jacket just to go next door, but if they went anywhere else for more decorations or flocking or whatever else they might need, she'd want it.

No matter how slowly she moved, it still took her less than ten minutes to reach the other door and knock.

Dean opened the door and stood off to the side. "Come on in."

"Thank you." She brushed past him but didn't let herself breathe as she did. She'd already caught a whiff of his cologne the night before and again as the door opened. She didn't need a full measure to know it had turned into her new favorite.

"Thanks for helping me eat all of this." He motioned to a table full of containers. "I didn't realize I ordered a family meal from that BBQ place in Serenity Landing."

"You didn't realize they were charging you a fortune?" She laid her jacket on the oversized chair.

He shrugged. "I live in Manhattan. Before that I lived in Hawaii. Everything is expensive in those places."

She would have noticed in a heartbeat, but she guessed it made sense.

Heading upstairs to the kitchen, Wendy found the plates and silverware. "Do you have drinks? Or do you want a bottle of water?" There were always some in the refrigerator, along with snacks and coffee grounds stocked in one of the cabinets.

"Water is fine. The coffee should be almost ready."

A sniff told Wendy the cologne wasn't the only thing making the place smell wonderful. The coffee was too.

Dean took the plates from her and set them on the table near the kitchen then started to move the food. Wendy poured herself a cup of coffee and grabbed a water out of the refrigerator.

Once seated, Dean said a quick word of prayer, taking Wendy by surprise. She didn't know many people who prayed out loud with someone who was basically a stranger.

"How did you get them to deliver out here? They don't normally." Pork-n-Stuff was her favorite, but it took at least twenty minutes to get there.

He ducked his head. "I offered a huge tip. The diner was really good. I ate there last night, which is where I heard about the loft, but I really wanted some good barbecue."

"I eat at the diner all the time, but I understand craving this." She took one of the buns and put some pulled pork on it before drizzling it with sauce. "It's fantastic."

"That's what Gavin said."

"Who's Gavin?" She cut the sandwich in half to make it easier to eat.

"Gavin Parmiggiano. He and his family live in Serenity Landing. He's worked for me for about five years." He shook his head. "His family comes to see me in the city a couple of times a year. He and his wife have been trying to convince me to move here for a while, but I'm not sure it's the best place."

"Why not?" She took a big bite.

"My ex-wife is in prison in Missouri." He sighed and stared at the sandwich he'd made. "It's a long story, but basically, she voluntarily terminated her parental rights long before I met her. After we got married, she kidnapped her daughter because her ex refused to hand their daughter over," he went on. "I didn't know she'd terminated her rights and thought Gavin was keeping her daughter from her. After I found out the truth, Gavin and I talked. We hit it off, and he had skills my company needed."

That was a lot to take in. "If she's in prison, why does it matter?"

Something about him had seemed familiar all along, but now even more so. Had she heard about a little girl being kidnapped a few years ago?

"I don't like being in the same state as her. It just reminds me of how I let my normally good judgment get clouded by a pretty face and great figure." He took a bite of his sandwich but still didn't look at her.

Wendy took another bite and thought over what he'd said. "I think we all make mistakes in judgment. It comes with being human. I know I've trusted people I shouldn't in the past. Nothing quite so dramatic, but it happens to the best of us."

In a move that surprised her, Wendy reached over and covered his hand with her own. "But I think you'll find that most people, in this part of Missouri at least, are worthy of your trust. It might be a bit harder to open yourself back up to dating again, but the people? They've got your back."

The warmth flowing from his hand to hers, up her arm, and straight to her chest, made her wish that he was ready to date again.

And that he'd pick her.

CHAPTER 3

Long before the star went on top of the tree, Dean decided he wanted to spend more time with Wendy. Even though his mind tried to talk him out of it. And really, his heart was conflicted. His ex had done a number on his ability to trust any woman.

He was shocked he'd trusted her with as much of the story as he did. There was more to it, of course, but he rarely told anyone about it.

It had been all over the news when it happened - in part because of his tech empire and in part because he'd been considering a Senate run.

His ex thought that, after a single term in the Senate, he could step into the presidency with her as First Lady. To do so, she needed her daughter back.

And, clearly, the best way to do that was to kidnap her.

"There. What do you think?"

Dean looked up from where he was holding the ladder to see the star lit up on top of the tree. "It looks great."

Wendy leaned her hip against the ladder. "What about the top section of the tree? Does it need more ornaments? Less?"

He stared at the top of the tree critically. Were there too many ornaments on one side versus the other? "I think it's fine." He really didn't care that much, except that it seemed almost like false advertising to have photos of Christmas decorations then not have them. He'd be here for several more days, and it was only a week and a half until Christmas.

"Okay." She carefully climbed down the ladder. "Now we're going to put garland on the staircase railing with some white twinkle lights wrapped in with it."

With a bounce, she landed on the floor. "And then, we'll need to put up the second tree downstairs."

"How big is the tree downstairs?" He really didn't want to put up another fifteen-foot tree. He wasn't sure he wanted to put up a six-foot one.

"Seven feet, but it's a lot easier than the other one."

He stifled a groan.

"If you don't want to help, you don't have to." Wendy looked over her shoulder as she headed for one of the boxes of decorations. "I don't mind doing it. I just haven't had time."

"I'll help. I really don't mind. It's been years since I put up a tree of my own."

She tilted her head. "You don't decorate?"

"I don't do it myself. I've not really noticed them much in recent years," he admitted. "Holidays aren't really my thing."

Wendy perched on the edge of the couch. "How come? Do you not spend them with your family?"

Dean shrugged. "I don't really have any family left. I'm an only child, and my parents passed years ago."

"And you don't have any friends who've invited you over?"

Did this conversation have HEA TV movie written all over it? "Nope. I spend most holidays traveling. I travel commercial and make sure to leave big tips for the people who deserve it."

She leaned forward a bit. "What about those who don't deserve a big tip but are still working holidays?"

He hadn't always considered that, but did the last few years. "I usually still tip them, just not as well, but really it depends. There's a difference between being upset or melancholy about working on Christmas and being rude and unpleasant."

"True."

Dean had already decided to leave her a large tip when he left. "Are you getting hungry? Is there some place nearby that I should make sure to try?"

"I'm not hungry, but yeah. There are some great places in Serenity Landing. Not as much here in Trumanville besides the diner and the bakery." She started for the storage room off to the side. Hoisting a box in one hand and a plastic bucket with ornaments by the handle in the other, she walked toward the stairs.

Before she reached them, Dean hurried to her side and took the tree box from her.

"Thanks."

Once downstairs, they worked together to set up the tree.

"I still can't believe you didn't know that trees come pre-lit these days," Wendy told him as she plugged it in.

He couldn't see her face, but suspected she was trying not to laugh. "I told you. I haven't put a tree up in years. My housekeeper does it or hires someone to do it. I'm pretty sure she hires someone to do the outside lights." It was a rooftop. It wasn't like he had groundskeepers to do it.

She groaned as she stood and stretched her back. "That reminds me that I need to get someone to volunteer to put the lights up outside this week."

"Volunteer?"

"Normally, my grandparents pay someone, but things are a bit tight." She gave a slight shrug. "I'll post on social media, and someone will volunteer. That's the way things are in a small town."

"That's great." He wondered how she'd react if he offered to pay for it. He guessed not too well.

She pulled her phone out and typed something in. "There. I bet I'll have it taken care of in an hour or so."

"Good." As they started putting ornaments on the tree, he asked about local holiday traditions.

"We have a parade and Christmas festival. I'm trying to finish getting ready for that. I still have half a dozen windows to paint, plus finish a bunch of stuff to sell at the booth." She hung a cartoon character on the tree and stared at it critically before moving it.

"What kinds of things do you make?"

"I do a lot of gift tags and hand painted signs." She pointed to the signs hanging up the wall by the staircase. "I did all of those."

He'd already studied them. They were excellent work - some kind of calligraphy with a line or two from old hymns. "They're great. I'm impressed. I don't have that kind of talent. Not even a little bit. There's not an artistic bone in my body."

Dean hung up a couple of ornaments, but Wendy reached for one of them.

"That one goes over here," she told him as she hung it near the one she'd just moved. "They're a set."

He stared down at her and when she glanced up at him, he thought about kissing her.

So why didn't he?

SETTING her small folding table in front of the bakery, Wendy tried to get that near kiss out of her head.

Thankfully, Dean's phone rang before they had to actually make a decision about whether or not to kiss.

She'd finished the tree while he went upstairs to conduct some business. By the time he returned, the moment was long over, and neither of them spoke of it. Instead, she bragged about the town coming to her rescue. The Beach brothers would put the outdoor lights up in the next day or so.

Painting the bakery window wasn't on her agenda for the day. She'd planned to do it in the morning, but she found herself too restless to sit at home and work on other projects.

Instead, she changed into her painting clothes, grabbed her cart, and loaded it with her plastic tub with her paints and brushes, her water cup, a step stool, then wheeled it across the street.

Stepping back to the curb, she stared at the windows and tried to decide exactly what she was going to put on them. This year's theme was winter wonderland, though they'd had precious little snow so far.

Another year had been tinsel and trees. The year before was gingerbread people. She had no idea what they were talking about for the next year.

It didn't matter.

This year needed snowmen and snowflakes and whites and blues.

After another moment of contemplation, she squeezed a big glob of white paint onto a plate and started her first snowman.

"What are you doing?" The bakery owner poked her head out the door. "I thought you weren't doing that until tomorrow."

Wendy shrugged. "Decided to do it tonight." The base snowball had taken form. "Do you have anything you definitely want or definitely don't?" They'd talked about it briefly and the other woman hadn't given her much direction.

"Not really. Just make it the best one on the block."

Wendy grinned at her. "They're all the best one on the block."

"What are you doing on the BnB windows?"

That was a great question. "I don't know that I'm going to do the windows. I've got a lot of other things to do." Main Street Boutique would be done in the morning. That definitely needed a special touch.

Mrs. Smith frowned. "They have to be done or else it won't look right."

"I'll try." The top of the snowman took shape. "We'll see." She could at least get a few hills of snow on them.

"How's that handsome hunk of a man who's staying there?" Mrs. Smith leaned closer. "He's been in and tipped so well I could have closed for the rest of the day."

She started on a hill the second snowman would sit on. "That's nice." How much money did that guy have? If he traveled on holidays and tipped really well, and tipped the bakery that much, he had to be loaded.

"Have you spent any time with him?"

"Not really. He's in town on business."

Would Mrs. Smith ever leave her alone?

"Don't forget to put mistletoe over a couple of them," Mrs. Smith went on. "Maybe one of them could be a bit bashful about it."

So much for not having any thoughts about it. "That sounds like a fantastic idea."

The phone inside rang giving Wendy a reprieve. It took a while, but eventually, the white was done. Hills of snow with white balls of snow were ready to be touched up and detailed.

As she worked, an idea for the KrazBnB windows came to her. If she could find the time to get it done.

The bakery closed long before she finished. She continued working, finishing with the mistletoe.

"I didn't know snowmen kissed."

Wendy turned to find Dean standing there. "I have no idea if they do or not, but she wanted mistletoe so she gets mistletoe."

She used red to make the ribbon holding the sprig.

"This is amazing," he told her. "Really fantastic."

"Thank you."

"Would you like to grab a bite to eat?" he asked.

Wendy stepped back to look at the windows. Did they work?

With a nod, she decided they did. "Let me get everything put away then change clothes." She used her water cup to rinse the last paintbrush she used.

To her surprise, Dean helped her put her things away then pushed the cart back across the street for her.

She parked it in the laundry room. The building had four doors. Three went into rooms on the lower floor. One went to stairs that led to the upper story and one of the lofts.

Two of the three remaining doors went into lofts. This one led to a laundry and storage area and then had another door that led to the apartment Wendy shared with her sister.

Stashing the cart in the laundry area, she hurried into the apartment and changed into something less paint-spattered.

When she walked back outside, Dean was staring at the bakery window across the street. He glanced both ways then trotted back over to her side.

"That's really incredible," he told her. "I can't do anything artistic."

They started to walk toward the diner. "I studied art education in college. I taught art for a while in Spring Meadow. It's about an hour-and-a-half from here near the Time Trek and Creature Quest theme parks."

"I've heard of them, but I've never been."

"You're missing out. We get passes every year. But anyway, my grandparents needed someone to come help out, so my sister and I moved back so we could. I've been substitute teaching and doing art lessons and the Painting with Pals classes."

"Are you going to teach full time again?"

"If I can get a job. This year, we didn't know about my grand-parents needing help until late so there weren't any in this area. The art teacher at Trumanville is retiring in a couple of years. I might be able to get that job." She shrugged. "The insurance is nice, but otherwise, I'm not sure I want to go back to teaching full-time. I really like doing the artwork and stuff, but it's not enough to pay the bills on its own yet."

Dean held the door to the diner, one she'd already decorated, for her. "Maybe we could look at what you charge? If you're not charging enough, that could be an easy way to bring in more income."

"Or a way to bring in no income," she challenged. "If I price myself out of what the local vendors are willing to pay, then I make nothing, even if someone could make an argument that I don't charge enough."

"Good point," he agreed as they sat in one of the booths.

Wendy took a sip of the water the waitress dropped off.

"But we can still look at your business plan and maybe figure something else out."

She snorted so hard water came out her nose. Mortified, she stared at Dean who stared back.

Great. What had she done?

It took everything in him not to laugh at her when she snorted water.

"I'm not sure what's funny about looking at your business plan." He took a sip of his own water.

She coughed into a napkin, likely trying to discretely wipe the water off her face. "I just love that you think I have a business plan. Mostly it's more a business prayer - as in *Dear God, please let us make enough to pay the bills.*"

"Does it work?"

Wendy nodded. "Mostly. I substitute teach. I paint windows. I do custom signs and chalkboards." She tilted her head toward the board above the window to the kitchen. "I did that one and a couple of others in here."

"Like the chalkboard with the specials outside the bakery?"

"That's mine," she confirmed.

"You do great work." He'd hire if he could, but he wasn't sure he had any actual need for chalkboard signs.

"Thanks."

The same waitress he'd had the other time he'd been in walked over. She rested a hand on Wendy's shoulder. "How're you doin' today, Wen?"

"Busy, but good. Nana and Papa are doing better, but getting ready for the festival is falling mostly on me this year."

"What about the home tour?" the waitress asked.

Wendy groaned and lowered her head onto her folded arms. "I'd forgotten about that. Nana usually organizes it, but with her being under the weather, it's probably behind."

"Let me bring you your favorite," the waitress crooned. "It'll be good. I have faith in you."

"Thanks." She didn't lift her head.

The waitress turned Dean. "And what can I get for you, sir?"

He'd been torn between two different choices the day before. This time he chose the other one.

By then Wendy was digging her phone out of her pocket. "I need to call Nana," she explained.

The call was short, but from what Dean gathered, Wendy would be going to her grandparents' house after the meal.

He was going to ask her about this home tour, but instead they ended up talking about life in a small town as they ate.

Dean still didn't understand the appeal.

"I don't get big cities," Wendy countered. "I've never been to New York, but I have been to several other large cities. I have a friend from here in town who married a guy from New York. They split their time these days, but he sees the appeal of the small town. When he's fundraising for charity, though, he can bring in a lot more in a big city. If you don't want to get run over by a taxi? Come to a small town."

He laughed. "Okay. I'll give you that the odds of being run over by a taxi are much smaller in Trumanville, but mostly that's because you don't have any taxis."

"Touché."

The waitress took their plates and gave them the check. He knew from his prior experience it could be split at the register, but instead he took some cash out of his wallet and tossed it on the table. "Come on. I'll take you to your nana's, and you can tell me all about this house parade thing."

Wendy looked like she wanted to protest, but decided not to. "I might need your help," she admitted as he unlocked the car with a click.

"Why is that?"

"With the flu going around town, everyone's being extra careful. They're talking about doing a virtual component to the Tour of Homes, instead of just an actual tour like usual. That way if someone is sick or recovering, they don't have a ton of people in their house."

He checked over his shoulder despite the excellent rear view camera display in the center of the dash. "Good plan."

"And none of us have any idea how to do virtual stuff. You seem like a techy guy, and I'm hoping you might be able to help. I'll throw in some free nights at the BnB if you do."

He glanced over to see her biting her bottom lip.

"The free nights aren't necessary, but I appreciate the offer. Why don't we talk to your nan and then we'll see what happens from there?"

"That would be great."

She pointed him in the right direction to get to the house, but it wasn't far. Off the main downtown area was a street full of old, stately houses.

"These were all built in the late 1800s," she told him as she pointed toward a drive. "They're all amazing inside, and the owners decorate them so well every year. This year, I'm doing windows for a few of them, but that's not terribly common for the houses. It's more a business thing. It can be a lot harder, too. Especially if one of the owners wants a window but has a much more elegant theme. Elegant isn't really my jam when it comes to painting windows."

"You have a more cutesy style?" he asked as he put the car in park.

"Definitely."

They walked up the sidewalk to the door. Before they knocked it opened and an older woman pulled Wendy in for a hug.

"Thank you for coming, dear. We're not contagious. At least that's what the doctor said. No fever for a few days but still recovering."

The woman let her go and turned to Dean. "And who are you?"

He held out a hand. "My name is Dean, ma'am." Had he told Wendy his last name? He didn't think so, and he kind of liked being relatively anonymous.

"Dean is a tech guy," Wendy told her grandmother. "You said you wanted to do mostly virtual tours this year. He's the guy who can help make that happen."

He appreciated her faith in him, but he wasn't sure it was actually the case. Not with the limitations of the small town. In New York? No problem.

Trumanville?

Well, that remained to be seen.

CHAPTER 4

By the time they left her grandparents' house, Wendy felt much better about the plan for the Trumanville Home Tour.

Given the flu running rampant through the area, those who wanted to attend the Trumanville Home Tour as usual could enter for a chance to do the regular home tour. If they won, it would cost ten dollars to tour. Those who didn't win or who didn't want to do the in-person tour, could do the virtual tour for five.

As always, proceeds would go to the local historical society.

"Are you sure you can do the digital tours?" Wendy asked as Dean drove them back toward downtown.

He chuckled. "Piece of cake. I'll have to get some equipment sent in unless I can get my hands on it locally. Gavin can probably help."

"Like what? Maybe I know someone who has what you need."

Dean rattled off a list of things that sounded like computer equipment.

"Uh, yeah. I'm no help." She glanced over at him. "But let me ask Cole. He's a fancy New Yorker. Maybe he knows where to get that stuff."

With another laugh, Dean pulled into a spot next to the Kraz-BnB. "I can get it by tomorrow or the next day. The videos don't need to be done until next week, right?"

"No. The Tour is Saturday. The parade and festival are during the day then the Tour is that night. Usually, tickets are sold only on Saturday during the festival." She climbed got out of the car, her mind still going. "We can sell the tickets until about half an hour before the festival ends, then do the drawing a few minutes later."

"How many people usually do the tour?" He stood next to her at the door to the laundry area.

Wendy shrugged. "I have no idea. Dozens and dozens?"

"Not hundreds?"

She snorted but no water came out this time. "No. Maybe a hundred, but that's about it. This is a small town, though we have quite a few lovely older homes and some newer homes that go all out to be on the Tour. We do attract people from all over, though. Maybe it is hundreds. Or at least one-fifty. I really have no idea."

"What are you doing tomorrow?" He took a half-step closer.

"I have some windows to get done and work to finish to get ready for the festival." She rested a hand on the door knob she'd already unlocked. "I'm not sure how long all of that will take, but probably most of the day."

He looked hopeful, but she had to correct him.

"Like all day. From the time I wake up to the time I go to sleep. I have two sets of windows to do. That's like six or seven hours. The rest of the day I'll be working on signs and gift tags and things like that." She wrinkled her nose. "Substitute teaching pays better, or at least more guaranteed, but I'm kind of glad the schools decided to take the week off."

"I don't blame you. Sounds like you have a lot on your plate."

Did he move closer or was it her imagination?

"But you'll still need to eat. Let me bring you dinner whenever you're ready for it?"

She needed to ask Madi Beach about meet cutes and smoldering eyes. Surely Madi - the town writer - would know.

Because she was pretty sure she'd now seen smoldering eyes in person.

Wendy nodded. "All right. I'll let you know when I think I'll have a break."

She wondered if he might move closer and kiss her, but instead, he took a step backward and smiled.

"I'll see you tomorrow then." He tipped an imaginary hat toward her. "Sleep well."

Wendy managed a smile, barely, through the butterflies that had suddenly taken up residence in her abdomen. "Thank you. You, too."

He winked at her before turning to go back to his loft.

Inside, Wendy did nothing but quickly get ready for bed and collapse. If she was going to get the windows done during daylight hours, she couldn't sleep half the day away.

By nine the next morning, she'd eaten breakfast, done her morning devotional, worked on several signs that would need to dry between layers, then gathered her things to do the windows on the antique store.

As she got her first paint brush ready, she realized someone was watching her.

Wendy turned to see Dean standing there with his hands in his pockets.

"How can I help?"

She blinked. No one had ever asked her that before. "I'm not sure you can. Unless you know what you're doing, it's really a job for just the artist."

"How about I get you a cup of coffee or hot chocolate to keep you warm while you work?"

The thought made her grin. "That you can do."

He winked at her again and sauntered off.

Two winks in two days? Had she ever been winked at before in her life?

Shaking her head, Wendy tried to focus on creating snowmen. These snowmen would have outdoor antiques.

Somehow.

She didn't quite know how yet.

No mistletoe this time.

Dean came back about the time she finished painting the snow on the ground at the bottom of the window.

He tilted his head. "It just looks like white lumps."

Wendy started on the bottom circle of a snowman. "I'll add detail later. It won't look like that when I'm done."

"I trust you."

"Good." She wiped the white paint on her thumb onto her shirt. This is why she wore old shirts despite her suspicion that Dean would show up at some point. Practicality outweighed her desire to wear something more flattering than a Trumanville Tigers shirt she'd had since her freshman year of high school.

After a sip of hot chocolate, she got back to work.

She didn't expect Dean to stick around, but he chose to, sitting either on her step stool or the stepladder, whichever one she wasn't using.

At times, companionable silence rested between them, but the rest of the time, they talked about anything and nothing and all of the things you talk about when you're starting a new relationship - whether it's a friendship or something more.

Wendy didn't know which one this would be, but she hoped for something closer to the "more" end of the spectrum.

The real question was what did Dean want?

If the winks were any indication, maybe it wasn't all one-sided.

THERE WERE a few meetings Dean should have joined via video-conference, but instead, he'd blew them off and spent the day shadowing Wendy.

Their conversations weren't deep or overly meaningful, but they laughed a lot, and he learned about her.

About life in a small town.

He was on the verge of admitting, albeit grudgingly, that maybe small-town life wasn't as bad as he'd thought.

Though he wouldn't want to move permanently. Probably.

With the right incentive he might be able to be convinced to spend a fair amount of time there, though he'd have to keep a place in the city for work. Much of his work could be done from anywhere, though.

Didn't Wendy say one of her friends married a New York businessman and they split their time between New York and Trumanville? Could he do the same?

Dean shook his head as Wendy wiped the paint off her hands with some baby wipes. He was getting a few giant steps ahead of himself.

"Why don't we grab lunch before your next window?" He hoped she would agree.

"Sure." She put the lid on her container full of paint bottles. "Can we grab something at the bakery though? I don't have enough time for the diner."

"Your wish is my command."

She left her cart sitting next to the antique store and started to walk down the sidewalk.

Dean didn't move, but looked from her to the cart. "You're not worried about it being stolen?"

Wendy laughed as she rolled her eyes and came back, linking her arm through his.

It caused his heart rate to spike, but not because it bothered him.

This was something else altogether.

"No. This isn't New York or any other big city where if someone were to take it, no one else would know the difference. Here, everyone knows it's mine so if they see anyone else with it, they'd say something."

Not the worst thing, he supposed.

Inside the bakery, the owner and Wendy were immediately engrossed in a conversation about the tour.

"I don't understand how virtual tours work," the owner said.

Wendy leaned in and lowered her voice. "I don't either, but this guy here..." She pointed to Dean. "He's a tech guru the likes of which Trumanville has never seen. He's got it all under control."

Dean laughed. "I don't know about tech guru..." Except he kind of was. "But it'll be online. You'll be given a code to access the website then you click on the house you want to tour. You can do the full tour start to finish or choose individual rooms. Zoom in if you want to see more detail and out if you want to take it all in."

Wendy frowned, but only for a second. "See? It'll be super easy."

The owner wasn't done fretting. "I don't know if my internet can do that."

"Can you stream MyBingeFlix?" Dean asked her.

"Well, yes."

"Do you have a computer? Or a smartphone?" he pressed.

"Yes."

He smiled at her. "Then you'll be fine." There had to be an app he could use if he needed to so it would be more readily accessible for those who didn't have a computer hooked up to the television but did have a streaming device.

With a quick text to his assistant, it would be taken care of.

"What is your name young man?" The owner narrowed her eyes at him.

"Dean, ma'am."

"Dean what?"

"Uh, just Dean is fine." He didn't have security with him like he usually did, on the condition that he keep to himself and didn't tell anyone who he really was.

There was a local guy who did security for a bunch of bigwigs he could call if needed. Maybe Jonathan knew some local video people who could help him get the tour ready to go. Between himself, Jonathan, and Gavin, surely they could figure something out.

He pulled his phone out and sent the text to his assistant, asking for help with both the technical side of things and getting in touch with the local guy.

The owner and Wendy had moved on to discussing the big movie premiere the weekend before.

"What are you going to do with the windows on the BnB?" the woman asked.

"I have a plan, but I don't know when I'll get to it. I've got a lot going on."

"Oh, but you need to!" The woman pleaded with Wendy. "Your building can't be the only one with windows that aren't decorated."

"I'll get them done."

Dean could hear the weariness in Wendy's voice despite the smile on her face. What could he do to make her life easier?

Except for getting the virtual tours ready, he didn't know. Most of the things she needed help doing were things that required artistic talent and not just throwing money at it.

The money thing he could do.

Artistic? Notsomuch.

Once they'd grabbed a sandwich and a drink, they went outside to sit on a nearby bench. The day was clear and cold, but not too cold. Sitting outside wouldn't be too uncomfortable.

They talked some more as they ate. Dean finished before Wendy and stretched his legs out in front of him, his arms finding their way along the bench on both sides.

"Let me take you to dinner Sunday," he said suddenly.

"What?" She covered her mouth with her hand as she realized she'd just taken a bite.

"The parade, festival, and tour are on Saturday. You can't get rid of me before then, and I'll help however I can. But Sunday, it'll all be over. Let me take you to dinner."

She finished chewing and swallowed. "Like a date?"

He chuckled. "Exactly like a date. Where would you like to go?"

"Um..." Wendy blinked at him. "I have no idea. It's been a hot minute since I went on a real date."

Dean laughed again. "A hot minute?"

"Quite a while. Longer than I care to admit."

He rubbed a thumb along her shoulder. "Well, I haven't been out on a real date since my ex-wife went insane, so you've probably been on one more recently than I have."

She leaned into him. "Probably. It sounds nice. Let's plan on it."

CHAPTER 5

G reat. Now Wendy had days to worry about what to wear instead of maybe twenty-four hours.

What to wear. What she'd say. What to do if he tried to kiss her.

It had been far too long since she'd had to worry about any of those things, and she wasn't crazy about it now.

By the time she was almost finished her second window painting of the day, she knew Dean better than she had before.

She knew he was a successful businessman, though she wasn't sure what exactly he did. Something with tech, it seemed, though she hadn't quite gotten a handle on what.

As she laughed at something he said, his phone buzzed. Dean excused himself while she continued putting the finishing touches on a Christmas tree. She stepped back and looked critically at the front windows of the Beach Reads bookstore.

The snowmen were reading books and looked far more peaceful than life currently was in the Beach family - or so she understood. The parents were splitting up, and it was taking a toll on everyone in the family. But the store was still in business - at least for now, so that was good.

"That sounds great, Jonathan. Thank you." Dean returned to his spot near her. "I'll talk to you soon."

"Who was that?"

"A guy who lives near here. His name is Jonathan Cranston, and he's getting me some help with the video recordings for the tour."

"Jonathan Cranston?" Did she know that name? Wait. "Jonathan *Langley*-Cranston?"

Dean shrugged. "Maybe?"

"I knew he lived on the other side of the lake, but I don't think I know anyone who knows him." She swiped at her forehead with the back of her wrist. "He's pretty much as close to American royalty as you can get."

He tossed a couple of Skittles into his mouth. "Hm. Did his dad or someone run for president a few years ago?"

"I think so. His brother went missing like five years ago. It was this whole huge thing when he just vanished. He reappeared a few years later about the time Jonathan's adopted daughter wandered off and was missing for about eighteen hours I think." It had been all over the news, too. "That's all I really know about him, and that's only because it was the only thing the local news talked about and every other post on social media detailed the whole thing."

"Apparently, he also knows some tech guys. So does Gavin. We'll start filming houses tonight."

"Some of the residents don't finish decorating until the two hours between the festival ending and the tour beginning." She pointed to the window with the end of her paintbrush. "I have three more to paint."

"Right. We talked with all of the home owners and told them we needed volunteers to go first. Several did. We've got today and tomorrow already lined up. We'll talk to everyone else again tomorrow and work on the rest."

She leaned against the brick separating two of the windows.

"Thank you so much for taking the lead on that. It's so far out of my experience that I didn't even know where to start. I probably would have walked around with my phone and recorded it then put the super shaky videos in a private social media group."

He laughed, though she didn't get the sense he was laughing at her. "That would be one way to do it and wouldn't be the worst way to do the tour this year. I promise this will be better, though."

"I have no doubt." She went back to putting the final touches on the beach-y, bookish snowman theme.

She stepped back and looked at it, then stepped back a few more times until she was between cars parked on the street in front of the store. "I think it's done. What do you think?"

Dean walked around a car and came to stand behind her, so close she could feel his breath against the wisps of her hair. "I think it looks amazing," he whispered. "But not as amazing as you."

Wendy felt blood rush to her face. "Thanks."

"Jonathan told me the best place to go for a date, too. He hooked us up with reservations."

"Reservations?" She swallowed hard. "Where did you decide we should go that needs reservations?"

"Some Italian place between Serenity Landing and Springfield."

She closed her eyes then stepped away and turned to him. "Savarino's?" Her eyes stayed closed.

"I think so."

Wendy opened one eye just a little bit. "Not to be a downer, but Savarino's is one of the nicest restaurants in southwest Missouri. It's also one of the most expensive."

Dean gave her one of the grins she was coming to love. "I think I can swing it this once."

He didn't get it, but she wasn't going to be the one to tell him. Did she have something she could wear? An evening gown or cocktail dress or whatever it was that women needed to wear.

"Did you bring a suit with you?" Maybe that would get her out of it. "It's one of those suit-and-tie-not-optional-and-a-tux-isn't-out-of-place places."

His smile widened. "I'll manage somehow."

Great. That meant she'd have to find something. Maybe her sister had something she could borrow. Or Mia Beach. Or Lani. Mia was married to a for-real movie star, and Lani married an actual prince.

They were close enough to the right size. Maybe they had something she could borrow "Okay. Savarino's it is."

"Great." He started for the sidewalk. "Let's get you packed up. What else do you need to get done today?"

Wendy shook herself out of her stupor. "Work for the booth, mostly. I've got a workshop set up in one of the other lofts."

"Is there anything I can help you with?"

She thought about it for a second. "Maybe. Some of the porch signs need a base coat. You could do that, and I can do the designs on the top. They're all custom, not templates, so you wouldn't be able to help with that part."

"I'm happy to do the base coat then." He started to put her paints back in the storage container.

As Wendy packed up her things with his help, she tried to figure out how she felt about this whole thing.

Helping with her artwork.

A date at Savarino's.

And a smile she was starting to love.

Wendy wasn't sure how she felt about all of it, but if she could just make it through the next few days, she'd figure it out then.

AFTER MEETING with the men Jonathan and Gavin sent to help, Dean went to one of the houses to record.

He was buzzed through the security gates and a moment later pulled up to the house of Mr. and Mrs. Beach.

The woman who opened the door welcomed him inside.

"I have a couple of other guys joining me shortly," he told her.

"We'll let them in." She held out a hand. "I'm Mama Beach."

He shifted the bag on his shoulder so he could shake it. "Dean."

Her eyes narrowed. "I know you."

"You do?" Was he being found out? And was that a good thing, a bad thing, or neither?

"You ran for the Senate a few years ago, or started to, before your wife..." Mama Beach sighed and shook her head. "I remember that and praying so hard for that little girl." She pointed a finger at him. "And I stay at your BnBs when I go out of town."

Dean chuckled. "I'm glad to hear that."

"We're grateful you're here to help put this all online. It's part of everyone's favorite event of the year."

"I'm happy to help."

A buzz indicated that the rest of his crew were at the gate.

He had a nice chat with Mama Beach while they worked. She told him he'd be down the street in a couple of days to do her niece and nephew-in-law's house.

The crew Jonathan had sent left before him.

Mama Beach looked at him in a way that made him feel seen in a way he hadn't been for a very long time. Then she hugged him.

Dean had heard that hugs could be therapeutic, but he'd never really believed it.

Until now.

Something about this woman's hug seeped inside in a way nothing had in a very long time.

She squeezed him even more tightly before letting go and whispering. "You'll do nicely."

He wanted to ask her what she meant, but the garage door squeaked open at the same time.

"That would be my husband, Papa Beach." She shooed Dean away. "You need to get back to the loft and get some rest, young man."

With a laugh, Dean picked up his bag. "I haven't been called young man in quite a while. It was great to meet you, Mama Beach. Maybe I'll see you Saturday. Wendy doesn't know it yet, but I'm hoping she'll let me help with their booth."

"That would be wonderful. I doubt her grandparents are up to working all afternoon. Her sister will help, and they might show up, but I wouldn't expect them to be there very long."

He made a mental note not to let Wendy turn down his help. "Thanks, Mama Beach. I'll be sure you get a link when this is live."

By the time he made it back to the loft, Dean was ready to crash. Before he could, he needed to upload the video files to the server so others could start working on them in the morning. Once that was done, he made himself take a quick shower then flopped on the bed. Almost as soon as he did, he was out cold.

He woke later than he wanted to the next morning, but he'd sent instructions with the videos, so he wasn't too worried about it getting started. He'd seen that the other videos had been uploaded by the other teams before he made it back.

The next two days continued much the same. First helping Wendy however he could, then recording video for the walk-throughs.

By the time he went to bed Friday evening - or early Saturday morning - everything was nearly done. The last videos would be taken care of by his team on Saturday.

While he spent the day with Wendy.

They'd worked on getting the booth itself ready and decorated for the festival. The products would be loaded in before the parade started.

That's why he was outside in the blustery cold before dawn

had fully broken. She'd asked if she could store a few of the things in his loft. He'd readily agreed, something that would have shocked him a few days earlier.

That's not how KrazBnBs were run.

Dean doubted that she would have asked a different guest, not one she hadn't gotten to know.

Hadn't thought about kissing.

Or at least one who hadn't thought about kissing her.

A text from Wendy told him she was running late, but if he was awake and wanted to, he could take some of the items to the booth and leave them out of sight.

He did so but as he returned, he noticed something.

The windows on the building had been painted.

Snowmen adorned them all.

When had she done that?

They'd all still been bare when he returned home.

He thought.

Making a mental note to ask Wendy about it later, he took a couple more loads over to the booth and put them away.

By the time he returned from his third trip, she stood outside the door to his loft, two cups of coffee in her hand.

"Thank you," she said simply as she handed him one. "I owe you."

Dean shook his head. "You don't owe me anything."

"Well, you still have my gratitude."

"That I'll take." He winked at her, something that surprised even him, after doing it several other times since he met her. "When did you get the windows painted?"

She glanced up at him then back down. That's when he noticed how tired she looked.

"I worked on them last night. They're not as good or detailed as I'd like, but they're done. It works for now."

"It looks fantastic, but you probably should have gotten some more sleep."

That earned him a glare. "I don't need a mother," Wendy told him. "I know I was up late. I know I'm going to pay for it today. I also know I'm planning to sleep in as late as I can and still watch church online tomorrow, then nap, then get ready for our date. But it needed to be done. I got it done. Now can we move on?"

Dean nodded, but promised himself he'd keep a close eye on her. This was going to be a long day anyway. Being exhausted wouldn't help anyone.

CHAPTER 6

With a smile, Wendy handed a sack to Mrs. Lotson. "Thank you, ma'am."

"My pleasure, dear. Thank you for personalizing them. The grandchildren will love them." Mrs. Lotson took her sack and started for the next booth.

With no one else standing there, Wendy took the chance to slump in her seat and close her eyes for a moment.

"Are you sure you can't sneak home for a nap?" Dean asked.

Wendy shook her head. "No. If I go home to sleep, I'll be out for the night, and that won't work. Plus, I have to do the personalizations. After the in-person tours tonight, then I'll sleep. I plan to watch church online in the morning, but I'm not going to set an alarm. If I don't wake up, I'll watch it later." She struggled to hold back a yawn.

"Good plan. And let me bring you something to eat. Let me know when you wake up and what you want. I'll bring it to you."

She gave him a smile. "That would be wonderful." Her sister was still staying with their grandparents for a couple of more days. This way, Wendy wouldn't have to make anything for herself to eat.

"Then we'll go out for dinner tomorrow night."

She nodded, their date to Savarino's having slipped her mind. "That sounds great."

A customer she didn't know walked up to the booth. Wendy stood and greeted the woman, showing her some of what they had to offer. The woman bought an "established" sign that needed a name and year put on it.

Wendy had her fill out the form and made sure it was legible so she wouldn't get it wrong.

The woman paid, and Wendy got to work in the back of the tent. The Whitaker Family, Established 2020. She only had to do the last name and year, thankfully. The rest was already done.

It didn't take long, but the woman had moved on and said she would be back in a bit to pick it up. That gave it time to finish drying.

Meantime, Dean had sold a stack of gift tags that needed names. She looked over the list before the man left, just to make sure she didn't have any questions.

"Hey, Mr. Krazowski."

Wendy's eyebrows pulled together as she looked up to see a man with a girl holding each hand.

"Gavin, I thought I told you to call me Dean."

Wendy saw him glance at her and shift from one foot to the other uncomfortably. Why?

"Wendy, this is Gavin. He's one of the local guys who has been helping with the virtual tour."

She finished the card she was working on and stood. "Nice to meet you."

Krazowski. The name niggled in the back of her mind, but she couldn't figure out why it sounded familiar.

Dean spoke again. "Now, I know these two are Isabella and Audra, but who is who?" He leaned over the front table and rested his weight on his forearms to talk to the girl who was walking.

"Can you tell yourselves apart? Or do you have your name written on the bottom of your foot?"

The little girl laughed. "I'm Izzy." She pointed at the girl on Gavin's other side. "That's Audra. Katie and Micah and the babies are with Mama."

Gavin chuckled. "One of the babies just turned three. The other two are actually babies." He winked at Wendy. "Apparently, twins run in my wife's family."

Wendy grinned. "Sounds like there's never a dull moment at your house."

"Nope. Not even a little bit."

She pulled out the Baby's First Christmas ornaments sheet. "Audra and Izzy, can you pick out one for each of your family members? Pick one you think they'd like, not the ones you like best. I think your mama needs one for each of you, don't you? They'll be my Christmas present for her."

"That's very kind of you, Wendy." While the girls huddled over the sheet, Gavin looked around and then pointed at one of the Established signs. "I do think I'd like that one, too."

Wendy laughed. "There's no obligation. Honest."

"I know." He pulled his walled out of his pocket. "But my wife pointed out one not too long ago. Dean, any chance you can hold onto it for me? I can get it from you before you leave, but there's no way I'd be able to hide it today."

Dean laughed. "Of course."

Gavin filled out the form while the girls pronounced they'd made their choices.

Wendy helped them choose the correct ones off the spinning rack. They needed help writing down the names and years. Gavin let them do the writing but helped with the spelling and numbers.

"Would you like these now or would you like to surprise your mama with them on Christmas?" Wendy asked the girls.

"Surprise!" they told her in unison.

"Then I'll put them with your daddy's sign, okay?"

The girls nodded eagerly as a girl a couple of years older walked up with a boy a little older still.

"Mom's ready to go," the boy told his dad. "The babies are almost ready to eat."

"Then off we go." Gavin tipped his head toward Wendy. "Nice to meet you. Thank you."

Wendy smiled back. "My pleasure."

"Bye, Mr. K!" The kid shouted as they started to walk away.

"Bye, Mr. K," Gavin echoed with a laugh. "I'll text you about picking that up."

"Sounds good."

"How do you know them?" Wendy asked, going back to finish the last couple of gift tags.

"The easy version is that Gavin works for me. Has for about five years now."

Wendy glanced up. "And the hard version?"

He sighed. "The hard version is a story for another time. The short version of it is that the girl who came up later? Katie?"

Wendy nodded.

"She's my ex-wife's daughter. The one she's in jail for kidnapping."

She felt her eyes go wide. "Oh. Right."

"He's a great guy. Kim..." He sighed. "She wasn't who I thought she was. Not even close. But she did give birth to a wonderful little girl. They come to see me in New York a couple of times a year. This is the first time I've been here. The babies are still pretty little, so I came to him this time."

A customer walked up to the table, pulling Dean's attention away from Wendy. She put the ornaments in a sack and attached it, along with the papers with the information on them, to the sign Gavin had chosen. She didn't need to do those right now if he wasn't going to pick them up for a few days.

She couldn't get the older girl out of her mind as she continued to work.

How scared that little girl must have been. How scared her father must have been.

How Dean must have felt realizing the woman he loved wasn't who he thought she was after all.

Maybe getting involved with someone who had such a complicated past wasn't the best plan after all.

AFTER THE PARMIGGIANO FAMILY LEFT, Dean could feel the atmosphere in the booth shift a bit. It wasn't just him, but Wendy, too.

Did seeing Katie affect her? It did Dean. He hadn't seen the little girl who should have been his step-daughter in nearly a year. She looked so much like her mother in some ways, though less so than she had a few years earlier.

Katie's hair had darkened to a medium brown rather than the blonde it had been when she was younger - and Kim's still was. Dean didn't think it came from a box or salon, but it wouldn't have been the only thing he had wrong about her.

A steady stream of customers kept his mind from wandering too far down that path. Wendy stayed busy working on personalizing purchased items.

The crowd dwindled as it neared five in the evening.

Wendy yawned and stretched. "Most folks are either heading home for dinner or waiting for the drawing. As soon as we get all of the remaining merchandise packed up, I need to get over to my grandparents' house."

"Can we start putting it all away?" Dean counted less than a dozen people on the street.

She sat on her chair with her shoulders slumped as she stared out at the streets. "Yeah. I doubt we'll get many more."

Together, they packed everything into boxes or totes then took down everything that wasn't part of the booth itself.

By the time they finished, the announcements would have already been made and the festival was officially over.

They made a couple of trips over to the lofts and left everything in the laundry room.

Dean offered to drive to her grandparents' house, but as they arrived, Dean received a text from Mama Beach offering him the two live tickets she'd won.

Wendy had already gone inside.

After greeting her sister and grandparents, he turned to Wendy and explained the text.

"You go ahead if you want to," she told him. "I need to stay here."

"No, you don't," her grandmother insisted. "We're feeling much better. I've told your sister we don't need her here anymore either, but she refuses to listen."

"I'll be here in a couple of days for Christmas anyway," Wendy's sister called from the other room.

"Go," her grandmother encouraged. "We'll be fine. But feel free to start here if you'd like."

"Thanks." Wendy gave her grandmother a hug as her grandfather started to adjust the lights in the rooms to give the best feel.

For the next several hours, they went from house to house, including the ones Dean had already seen. Wendy admitted that, normally, she visited most of them on her own as a guest of the family or for a meal or other Christmas gathering so she'd never actually done the tour.

By ten, they'd returned to downtown. Wendy had smothered a few yawns but not as bad as Dean had thought she'd be.

"Thank you for taking me with you," she told him, one hand on the door as it stood slightly ajar. "It was fun."

"My pleasure. I've been keeping an eye on the website. The comments have all been good."

"That's awesome. Thank you again. It was a monumental task.

You probably should have been paid a very pretty penny and did it for nothing."

He gave her a soft smile. "It was no trouble." Not entirely the truth, but close enough. "And I don't need the money, so I'm glad I was able to help." Both the truth.

This time she didn't hold back the yawn. "Tomorrow, after I wake up, I'll do the ornaments and sign for your friends. Then he can pick it up, or we could drop it off on our way to dinner."

Dean couldn't help laughing. "That would kind of ruin the surprise, though, wouldn't it?"

She closed her eyes and let her head fall forward as she groaned. "Good point. I think I need sleep."

He reached out and rested a hand on her shoulder. "Go inside, change into your most comfortable pajamas, brush your teeth, and collapse. Text me when you wake up."

"That sounds perfect." She looked up at him.

Were those tears in her eyes?

"Thank you."

"My pleasure."

She looked straight in his eyes for a moment then went inside.

Dean went to the next door and let himself into the loft. He could hear the water running in one of the other units and presumed Wendy was taking a shower or bath. He smiled. Good for her.

He took a quick shower of his own then went to bed.

Since he wasn't nearly as exhausted as Wendy, Dean woke in time to grab breakfast on his way to the church Gavin had told him about.

He sat in the back but recognized several people who occasionally graced the tabloid racks at grocery stores. The people around them treated them like anyone else.

That made Dean feel more comfortable. He wasn't as recognizable as some, but his name was well-known.

Wendy hadn't seemed to put two and two together when

Gavin and the kids came up the night before, though. Dean chalked it up to her exhaustion. Eventually, she'd realize who he was.

That he owned a major hotel chain. A search engine and email service.

KrazBnB.

Among other things.

He made it back to his loft before he heard from Wendy. She said she'd noticed his car was gone and that she'd already grabbed some leftovers from the kitchen. She'd be ready to go when he was for their dinner.

He replied and said he'd pick her up about six. The drive to Savarino's wasn't as short as he'd like, but the reviews were excellent, and it came highly recommended.

Gavin had whistled when he mentioned it as they talked after the church service.

By five-thirty, Dean was ready to go. He wore his favorite suit with his favorite tie. Both were suitably neutral so he wouldn't clash with whatever color Wendy chose to wear.

Right at six, he left his loft and walked to her door and rang the bell.

A text from Wendy said she'd be there in a minute. With the laundry room in between, she likely couldn't be heard from inside the apartment itself and it certainly wasn't convenient to come to the door.

Several minutes later, he heard the inner door open then close.

He took a deep breath as he recognized the sound of heels tapping on the tile floor.

Here went nothing.

CHAPTER 7

Sometime during the night, the name clicked.

Dean Krazowski.

As in KrazBnb. KrazSuites. YadaYada email and web search.

As in more money than you could shake a stick at.

She didn't know what to do with that. When Wendy woke up, she was grateful to notice his car wasn't in front of the building like it had been the night before.

That gave her some time to sort through it all in her head.

Maybe.

If she could.

She wasn't sure she could wrap her head around who he was.

Or how much money he had.

Or what kind of dress she'd need to wear to match the suit he'd be wearing.

The little black dress she'd planned on wouldn't work, and she didn't really want to reach out to Mia or Lani.

She snuck out the back door and made a quick trip to one of the local boutiques. It was closed on a Sunday, but Wendy called in a favor.

Even better, there was a dress that had been returned and couldn't be resold for full price. Wendy was able to purchase it for a significant discount.

She returned to her apartment in time to take a shower and wash her hair then spend the time to make it cooperate, something she didn't do often.

Then extra care with her make-up. Finally, she slipped the dress on, running only a few minutes late. She could hear Dean walking around upstairs where his loft covered her apartment. Then she heard him walking down the stairs.

The zipper was a bit of a struggle to get fully zipped and fastened, but she managed to get that done before the knock on the front door sounded.

She took a few seconds to send a text message that she'd be there momentarily then found the shoes the boutique owner had loaned her from her personal collection.

With a final look in the full-length mirror, Wendy took a deep breath and headed for the door that led into the laundry room.

The first thing she saw was the sign she needed to do for Dean's friend. She'd forgotten about it and the ornaments. She'd need to do that when she got home - or maybe first thing in the morning.

Opening the door, Wendy pasted a smile on her face. As soon as she saw Dean, she knew the shopping trip had been the right move.

It looked like a blue suit, but Wendy suspected it cost more than her entire wardrobe - twice.

"Hey." Dean's smile widened as he saw her. "You look incredible."

"Thanks. You look pretty amazing, too."

He extended an elbow toward her. "Shall we?"

Wendy stepped onto the sidewalk and turned to lock the door. "You know, this is where we first met."

Dean laughed. "It is. I like this way of walking off the curb a little better." He opened the passenger door of his rental car for her.

A minute later, they were on their way to Savarino's. The drive would take a while.

"How did you sleep?" The car's GPS told Dean where to turn north.

"Best I've slept in a while," Wendy admitted.

"Good. I'm glad to hear that. I'm sorry I wasn't home to bring you something to eat."

She shrugged. "I had leftovers in the fridge. It was fine. What about you? Where were you?"

"I went to church in Serenity Landing with the Parmiggiano family. Well, not with them, but at their church. It was nice. Lots of Christmas carols. Old ones that I remembered from when I was a kid and a couple of new ones."

"I usually go to church in Trumanville. It's a smaller church than the one you probably went to, but I've been there my whole life. It's home."

"Makes sense."

"Mrs. Braverman was my Sunday school teacher all through elementary." Wendy smiled to herself as she looked out the window at the passing landscape. "She's been playing matchmaker for years. I'm surprised she hasn't tried to set me up since I've been home."

"Uh..."

She glanced over to Dean wincing. "What?"

"Mrs. Braverman is the one who recommended I check out the loft when my suite at the resort wasn't ready."

Wendy groaned. "You're kidding."

"Nope. We had dinner together my first night in town. There weren't any other seats in the diner. She even paid for it."

"So she didn't know who you are?" Wendy stared out the windshield.

"No. I tried to pay, but she refused to let me. I'll make it up to her some other way."

"I'm sure you will."

She could see him glance at her.

"That came out snarkier than I meant it to. I'm sure you will find a way to thank her."

"I've been thinking but haven't come up with a good way yet."

Several miles passed in silence until Dean broke it. "You figured out who I am, didn't you?"

"You mean the Kraz in KrazBnBs? And the hotels? And tech?" She looked down at her hands, though she couldn't really see them as the dark deepened. "Yeah. It hit me sometime overnight. I woke up realizing who you were. I'm kind of surprised you don't have an entourage."

"My security team isn't happy about it. I'm supposed to fly under the radar. I was put in touch with Jonathan Langley-Cranston. He runs a security firm. If I need it, I call him. He and Gavin helped me get a team together for the virtual tours."

"But no assistants? No valet? No stylist?"

Dean laughed. "No. I have been in contact with my assistant on a daily basis, but I'd planned to mostly take the rest of the year off. I just wanted to see Gavin and his family. I did have some things to talk with him about, but it could have been done over a video conference."

He tapped his fingers on the steering wheel. "I wanted to check on Katie. I worry about her. She's doing amazing but still."

Wendy waited for him to go on.

"When Kim and I were dating, she told me Gavin was keeping Katie from her. She wanted Katie to be the flower girl at our wedding, but Gavin never returned her emails or returned them with nasty ones. Turned out, Kim was sleeping with one of my VPs. They faked the emails."

She couldn't stop the gasp. "Oh no. That's awful."

He gripped the steering wheel so hard she could see his

knuckles turn white. "Yeah. Well, with all of that and the kidnapping. I worry about Katie. All of the kids have a college fund, though they don't know about it yet. I need to tell Gavin and Bethany. I was going to just set one up for Katie, but she adores her siblings. I couldn't single her out like that."

"That's incredible."

"The real problem, now, though, is that it's ruined my ability to trust women." He sighed. "I'm working on that, though."

He reached over and took her hand. "And I have you to thank for that."

WITH CURVES COMING up in the road, Dean couldn't take his eyes off of it long enough to do more than glance at Wendy.

"How did I do that? We've known each other a week."

He linked his fingers with hers. "I'm not really sure. I don't think you made some kind of concerted effort to bring my walls down or anything like that, but something about you made me want to drop them and get to know you better."

"I see."

The drive continued as did the silence.

Dean wasn't quite sure why. As he slowed to turn off Highway PP onto Highway 60 where it went through Serenity Landing, he paused long enough to let some cars go by and took a longer look at Wendy.

She stared out the window.

"Is it something I said?" he asked once he made the turn.

"Not really."

"Then why so quiet? Is something wrong?"

She sighed but didn't pull her hand away. "I'm trying to reconcile the guy I've known for the last week - sweet and helpful, clearly not broke but not throwing money around either - with the tech-and-hotel mogul who could buy the whole town of Trumanville without losing sleep over it."

"I'm still just me, Wendy." He rubbed his thumb along the back of her hand. "I'm the same person."

"I get that, but I also get that a life with you isn't going to be normal. The thought occurred to me a couple of times in the last week, just in passing. You know in that, 'Hey a guy asked me out on a date... do I think I might like him enough it could go the distance? If so, what would that look like?' kind of way. And whatever I thought that might be is completely different with a tech... magnate."

That made Dean chuckle. "I don't think I'm a magnate, but yes. There are certain aspects of my life that would be different than you might have thought. Some of them are good. Some aren't. Like needing security on a regular basis. But it also means I don't have to stand in security lines at the airport or worry about how much a trip to the Caymans or New Sargasso might cost."

"I have always wanted to go to New Sargasso," she admitted. "I loved *The Trilunium Chronicles* as a kid."

"I never read them. Those are the ones with the dragon, right?"

"Say it ain't so! But yes. They did all of the movies starting about fifteen years ago. They found the sixth book late last spring, and it released a few weeks ago."

"I think I remember hearing something about that."

She shifted to look at him. "Where did you grow up?"

"Long Island. We were comfortably middle class. We didn't worry about food or rent but didn't take big vacations very often. That kind of thing. We'd go to the city to see a show from time to time, but usually the cheapest seats or maybe a matinee."

Wendy straightened and looked at him more closely. "You could probably fly back to the city tomorrow and have tickets for *Hamilton*, couldn't you?"

David struggled to keep a straight face. "No. Even I can't get tickets to *Hamilton* tomorrow."

56

"Really?"

He grinned. "They don't do shows on Monday."

Wendy dropped his hand and smacked his arm. "But you could get them for Tuesday?"

With a laugh, he reached for her hand again. The GPS warned they were only a mile from their destination. "Probably. Definitely one day this week." He thought better of it. "Well, it's a holiday week, so maybe, maybe not. Would you want to go to the city with me and see it?"

Before she could answer, he turned into the parking lot of Savarino's. At the door, the valet took the car as Dean offered Wendy his arm.

Once inside, he gave his name to the maître d' and stood to the side to wait.

"I would like to go to New York sometime." Wendy leaned her head against his upper arm as her hand held the inside of his elbow. "Probably not this week because it's Christmas week and not New Year's either because it's so crazy, but sometime."

"Then I'll take you. I'll even make sure you get to see *Hamilton*."

"Honestly? I'd rather see *Come From Away* or *Wicked*. Or maybe *The Play that Goes Wrong*, but I think it's considered Off-Broadway."

He chuckled softly. "We'll figure something out after the first of the year."

"How long are you staying in Trumanville?"

Their name was called before he could answer, giving Dean a momentary reprieve. A moment later, they were seated at a table near the dance floor. It wouldn't have been his first choice, but since the place was almost full, he took what he could get.

As she looked over the menu, he could see her eyes widen slightly. She likely felt about the same way he did when he realized he could start affording things without worrying too much about it.

"Order whatever you want," he told her softly. "Please."

She nodded.

Ten minutes later, they'd ordered their meal.

"To answer your question from earlier, I don't know how long I'm staying in Trumanville. When do you have someone else scheduled for the loft?"

"I don't know." She pulled her phone out of her pocket and looked. "Today is the twentieth. I've got someone coming on the twenty-third. I guess that's when you have to be out." She sounded as sad as he felt.

"I guess so," he said softly.

"One of the other lofts is available for the next few weeks. It was booked starting tomorrow, but the renter messaged me this afternoon to cancel."

He took a sip of his water. "What's your cancellation policy?"

"Seven days or forfeiture of the first night plus half the fees. If it's less than three days, it's forfeiture of half the total." She didn't look at him.

"You refunded the whole thing, didn't you?"

Wendy nodded. "They used to live in Trumanville. I've known them most of my life. The husband had a heart attack last week, and she didn't think about canceling until today."

"That was very kind of you." He reached over and squeezed her hand. "And, if you'll have me, I'm happy to pay the last-minute rate on that loft through at least the end of the year."

CHAPTER 8

T
he words came as a relief to Wendy. "There is no last-
minute rate. It's the same as the regular rate."

"A holiday rate?"

Wendy shook her head. "Nope. We don't have any kind of big
festivals or anything that warrant a higher rate. Occasionally, we
do discount rates if it's extra slow. We have some local artists -
writers, mostly - who will rent one for a few days when we do
that. If we had something like... Sturgis, maybe, but we don't."

"You know you're leaving money on the table by not charging
more, right? I'm not saying double or triple the price but a
percentage for holidays isn't a bad thing."

"I know, but I just can't bring myself to do it. We don't have
that many people just dying to stay in Trumanville and most are
here to see family. I don't see the need to raise the price."

"Fair enough."

The waiter arrived with their salads.

They talked about a little bit of everything, but nothing deep
or important as they ate their salads then their dinner.

When they finished, Dean wiped his mouth on the cloth
napkin. "Would you like to dance?" he asked, holding out a hand.

Wendy hesitated. "I've never really danced with anyone before."

A slow grin crossed his face. "That's all right. It's been a long time since I have. At least this way we'll both be a bit awkward out there."

She rolled her eyes at him. "Fine."

He stood and helped her with her chair. A minute later, she stood in his arms as they moved slowly in time to the music.

Before she could stop herself, Wendy blurted out the question that had been weighing heavily on her mind. "How do you see a relationship working?"

"What do you mean?" His hand slid a little farther around her waist, moving her closer to him.

"I know you've been working some from here, but you also said everything was extra slow because of the holidays, so it wasn't a big deal for you to work from here because there wasn't much to do compared to normal."

He nodded, his chin ending up against her temple. "That's true."

"So if we start a relationship, how does it work? I wouldn't mind visiting the city pretty regularly, but I have no desire to live there. Could you live here?"

With his sigh, his breath moved the strands of hair that had escaped her hairdo. "I wouldn't mind. I don't know about being able to run my business from here regularly."

"So how would a relationship work?" The last thing she wanted was to get her heart involved only to find out there was no way it could work geographically.

"Airfare isn't an issue. One or both of us can go back and forth without any issue. Either on my plane, or I can send one for you. No standing in line or anything. Actual flying time is less than three hours. Less than driving to St. Louis. It's the security and everything else that takes so much time."

Wendy smirked. "And the direct flight. You can't get a direct flight from Springfield to New York. You have to layover in Chicago or Charlotte or Dallas or somewhere else."

"Good point." He spun her around. "So I spend work weeks in New York and come here on the weekends. If it's a weekend I can't come back for some reason, you can come see me. We'll go see shows or whatever else you want to do."

"And long term?"

"Why do we need to worry about long term at the moment? We'll see if things work out between us then go from there. I'd imagine that if things go the way we'd like them to, there will likely be a fair bit of back and forth even if our home base is in Trumanville."

Was that a kiss to the side of her head? Wendy wasn't sure. "I think I could handle that, but I think I need the trips to the city or other places to be the exception rather than the rule. Not every week or weekend. Is that even possible?"

"In theory."

That was definitely a kiss to the side of her head.

"But life can change over time. I'm definitely open to being based out of Trumanville or somewhere nearby. We can see where it goes from there. If things are working out, we'll talk more about it. I want to be able to make it work, but I just can't promise that I'll be able to spend as much time here as I'd like."

The song came to an end and Wendy stepped back a bit. "Thank you for being honest."

They went back to the table where he held her chair for her again.

"Where does that leave us?" he asked as the waitress left with his card to charge him for the meal - which was delicious, but probably not worth what he was paying for it.

"I don't know."

She was going to say something else but the waitress returned. He wasn't going to let it drop, she knew that, and she didn't want him to.

Wendy *wanted* to see where a relationship with Dean could go, but she also didn't want to get hurt.

She wasn't sure the two things were both possible.

"Did you want to stop and get some dessert on the way back?" he asked as he headed down Highway 60 toward Serenity Landing.

"How about the diner? They have an amazing chocolate cake." And it would buy her some time.

Dean reached over and took her hand. "That sounds fantastic."

The ride back was nearly as quiet as the ride there. Dean asked her questions about Serenity Landing as they drove through it then about the area in general as they continued down the dark roads toward Trumanville.

Throughout their dessert, he kept asking questions about her, about Trumanville, about the different businesses she was a part of. He offered valuable suggestions and insights, but never made her feel like she was stupid or that he was mansplaining anything.

If he explained something, it was because she genuinely didn't understand.

Then he walked her back to the door to the laundry.

His hand reached up to brush a bit of hair off her face and then he leaned down.

And kissed her.

IN THE TWELVE hours since Dean kissed Wendy in front of her door, he'd done precisely nothing except sleep, eat a quick breakfast, and go back to sleep.

He didn't know why he was so tired, except that maybe the last week and a half had caught up with him.

A knock on the door to the loft sounded from downstairs. With a yawn, he swung his legs over the side of the bed and grabbed his phone as he stood to make his way down.

At least he already wore a t-shirt with his pajama pants.

When he reached the door, he moved the curtains aside to peek out the window. It surprised him to see Wendy standing there.

He opened the door. "Good morning."

As she glanced at his clothes, she smirked. "It's afternoon, sleepyhead."

"What time is it?" He glanced at his watch. "So it is. But barely."

She held out a to-go cup. "I brought you coffee anyway."

He took it from her. "Thanks." Stepping back, Dean opened the door farther. "Come on in."

"I'm not bothering you?"

"Nope." Taking a sip of the coffee, he closed the door behind him.

She pointed over her shoulder with her thumb. "Would you like me to go get you something to eat? You've got to be starving."

"I'm fine. I ate earlier then went back to bed." He sat on one of the chairs in the first-floor living area and motioned for her to take a seat. "If you want to grab lunch in a bit, I could get dressed, and we could get something or have something delivered."

Wendy sank onto the couch. "Delivered sounds good."

He pulled his phone out. "Pizza?"

She nodded.

They'd talked about pizza enough over the last week to feel fairly certain he knew what she wanted, but he asked anyway. A moment later, he'd placed the order.

"Thank you for the coffee," he told her again before taking another sip.

"It's kind of a peace offering." She didn't look at him as she spoke.

"Peace offering? Are we fighting?"

"Not really, but I gave you a really hard time about the whole New York thing last night and not wanting to even try this without knowing how the living situation could work out eventually."

It hadn't been his favorite part of the evening, but it wasn't worth getting in a snit over. "I understand where you're coming from. If things do work out with us in the long term, the living situation would be something we'd have to discuss. I can't work fully from this area, but I would do my best to be here as much as possible. I'd like to be here a lot more often. Seeing the Parmiggianos reminded me how much I like seeing them, especially Katie. I've avoided it far too long."

"That's good to know."

"But that doesn't mean I won't have to be in New York or LA or somewhere else on a pretty regular basis. Even if I live here full time, I'll likely have to be out of town at least once or twice a month. I'm already out of New York at least once a month." He didn't want to scare her off, but he did need to be honest.

"I know. I understand that. There's no way to know if it'll work until we try. It could end up being too much, but I want to give it a shot."

It took a second for the words to sink in. "You want to try this? To try us?"

Wendy nodded but still didn't look at him. "I do. I want to visit New York and maybe another city or two or three where you go on business, but not in a row. Over the course of several months."

Dean chuckled. "I get that. New York can be overwhelming. Some of the other cities less so, but it's a lot of travel sometimes."

"So what do you think it'll look like?"

"I think it'll look like I'm here until the first Monday of the new year. I'll need to go back to New York that Sunday night or early Monday morning. I'll probably be there for at least most of January trying to wrap things up so I can move most of my personal work out here."

He'd thought about this a lot the last few days. "I can't just pick up and leave. If you want to come visit, you are more than welcome. Just let me know what dates work for you, and I'll either send my plane or charter one for you. I probably won't be able to take the whole time off work, but I'll make sure we have time together. You'll have a car to take you where you want to go or someone to help you get there so you don't have to navigate the city by yourself at first."

"Maybe Brittany will be there."

He tilted his head in confusion.

"My friend from here who married a New Yorker. They split their time, but their only child is a high school senior. Brittany took to the city a lot easier than I likely will. If she and Cole are there the same time I am, then we can maybe travel together, and she can help make sure I don't get lost and end up in Jersey or something."

Dean laughed. "That sounds perfect."

For twenty minutes, they talked, but it was different. The questions were much the same as their other light conversations, but the atmosphere this time was different.

Lighter.

Less uncertain.

The pizza arrived five minutes before the time they'd been given. Dean tipped extra well for that.

He carried it upstairs and set it on the bar. "I think I'm going to change," he told Wendy as she pulled plates out of the cupboard.

"Don't feel the need on my account," she told him, grabbing forks from a drawer. She pointed the tines over his head. "You might want to move, though."

Dean looked up.

Mistletoe?

"Where did that come from?" he asked.

"I have no idea," Wendy told him. "My sister came in one day last week and put up the nativity scenes, remember? Maybe she did it."

"Possible." A slow grin crossed his face. "But what if I don't want to move?"

She had to pass near him to get to the pizza. He caught her by the waist and pulled her close.

"What if I want to seal this plan of yours with a kiss?"

The look in her eyes softened. "I think that sounds perfect."

This time when he kissed her, neither of them hesitated or felt reserved.

Instead, it was a kiss of promise and potential.

The kind he'd waited his whole life to find. He'd thought he'd found it once.

But this time, Dean had a feeling it could be forever.

CHAPTER 9

A s the car drove from LaGuardia to Manhattan, Wendy wanted to take in the views, but there wasn't much to see. Either side of the roadway had barriers, likely to keep the sound out of the neighborhoods below.

"Mr. Krazowski asked me to take you on a bit more scenic route, ma'am." The driver still didn't look comfortable with her riding in the front seat of the town car, but she didn't want to sit in the back.

"I appreciate it." All she could really see was the highway, the occasional taller building, and, every once in a while, a glimpse of downtown Manhattan.

Coming in on the private plane, something she could get used to, the stewardess sat next to her and pointed out the landmarks they could see - Freedom Tower, the Statue of Liberty, and Citi Field where the Mets played.

"He thought you'd enjoy entering Manhattan over one of the bridges rather than a tunnel," he told her.

"Definitely."

They exited the highway to drive through a residential and

business neighborhood then over a rail yard before getting back on a highway of some kind.

A few minutes later, they were on a bridge.

"We'll go over Roosevelt Island in a minute," the driver told her. "Then into Manhattan."

"This is amazing." She leaned forward and looked at the underside of the metal structure above the roadway. "Sorry. I'm from a small town in the Midwest."

The driver chuckled. "I understand. It's the best city in the world, but it can be overwhelming, and there's definitely something to be said for miles of nothing, too."

She never did get a really good look at downtown and Freedom Tower from the ground. Dean promised to take her down there and to the Memorial while she was in the city.

The first two weeks of their new relationship had been pretty amazing. Dean stayed in one loft or the other until early the morning of January 4. They spent most of their time together. But the last six weeks...

Since he flew back to New York, they texted often but had only been able to talk for a few minutes most days as he tried to get everything ready for a part-time move to southwest Missouri.

Once a week, they scheduled a much longer video chat, but those hadn't been enough. She missed him more than she could have thought possible after such a short period of time.

He admitted to missing her just as much.

Then the car was off the bridge and on a street lined with apartments. In Springfield, they'd be considered skyscrapers. Here, they weren't even considered tall.

The driver pulled over into a makeshift parking spot and turned on his caution lights.

"Why did we stop?" She watched as those walking by they went about their daily lives. There weren't as many people as she would have expected, though the numbers were likely higher than on the streets of downtown Trumanville - and definitely more than anywhere else in town. They were bundled up far more than the folks back in Missouri.

A minute later another car pulled up in front of them.

Wendy gasped. "Is that Dean?"

The driver just smiled and opened his door, a blast of cold air making its way in. "Mr. Krazowski will drive you the rest of the way."

Dean clapped the man on the shoulder as he made it to the car. "Thanks, Frank."

Once inside with the door closed, he leaned over and gave her a soft kiss that made her wish they were already at his apartment - and, at the same time, glad they weren't. "Welcome to New York. I'm glad you're here."

She smiled and kissed him again. "I'm glad to be here. I thought we weren't supposed to kiss in public though."

He laughed as he reached around to put his seatbelt on. "Frank kept an eye out. There wasn't anyone around."

"I thought you were working."

Dean pulled the car back into traffic then reached over and took her hand. "My call ended early. I texted Frank when I realized it was wrapping up faster than I expected. Your flight had already landed, so I told him to find a spot to park when you made it over the bridge. We could find you from the GPS on the car."

They stopped at a light, and Dean kissed her again. "Plus, I wanted to see your first visit to the city myself."

As they drove on, she kept up a running commentary on what she saw, causing him to laugh at her fairly regularly.

A few areas had several buildings that looked more like downtown Trumanville storefronts. Brownstones, maybe? They were mostly three or four stories with stoops and stairs. Like every quaint street she'd ever seen in small town Missouri. But only a few buildings at a time back home. Not block after block.

Interspersed were small businesses like grocery stores and

restaurants, pizza places and parking garages, even a Buddhist Temple. Taller apartment buildings with eight or twelve stories looked more like something she'd seen on *Friends*. At some point she realized the street was one-way only, something she'd seldom experienced.

A few of the buildings even had names on the front. What would it be like to live in a building with a real name and not just "Trumanville Shoe Manufacturing" like the concrete façade in front of the lofts said?

"Would you be mortified if I came back with my camera and took pictures of, like, everything?"

He laughed. "I doubt you could mortify me so easily."

The buildings seemed to get consistently taller.

"Why do so many of the buildings have scaffolding in front of them?" she asked.

"Usually there's construction in or on the building. The scaffolding and the cover protect those on the sidewalk from falling debris."

"Makes sense." She tilted her head up to look out of the windshield. "It's taller than home, obviously, but not as tall as I would have thought."

"This is the wrong part of the city for the super tall buildings. You'll be able to see some of them when we get to the park and from my building."

He turned right and then a few minutes later, turned left again.

"So many one-way streets," she muttered.

They came to a stop at a light. In front of her were only trees and sky for as far as she could see.

"Is that Central Park?" she asked him.

"Yep. We're going to drive right through it, but you won't be able to see much. To the left is the zoo. We'll walk through most of it over the course of the next week." He'd promised he'd only work half days while she was in town.

All she could see was a rock wall with trees on top of it as they drove. He told her about what was on the other side of the walls and vegetation. She supposed it increased the illusion of being insulated from the city if you were in the park. They reached the stoplight at the other side of the park.

"Your building is the second one, right?" Butterflies started to take their spots in her stomach.

"Yep. You can't see it from here though. Not the way it's set back from 66th Street and with how tall the first building is."

She'd looked it up. There wasn't anything that could compare to the grandeur of his building. The entry alone was nicer than anything Trumanville could begin to offer. Not even Springfield had anything close.

The light turned green, and Dean eased his way through the intersection and, a moment later, pulled into a circle drive in front of the building.

Since the other car had made it through the light, Frank already waited to hold Wendy's door for her while Dean climbed out on his own.

Then he stopped. "Are you hungry?" he asked over the top of the car.

"I could eat."

"Let's go get some pizza. You said you wanted real New York pizza, right?"

She'd only mentioned it several times. "Yep."

"Let's go get some." He climbed back in the car, looking up at Frank. "We'll park at the Kraz Suites on Eighth Avenue and walk from there."

"Yes, sir."

The cars pulled back out of the drive.

As they drove, he explained that the numbered avenues went north/south and the streets went east/west. Broadway went diagonal.

They started down Columbus Avenue, but it turned into Ninth Avenue at some point.

She twisted in her seat to look at a corner restaurant. "Is that a the one from Seinfeld?"

Dean laughed. "No, but we can do a famous places in New York tour later."

"Like the *Friends* building?"

Another laugh. "Sure."

SOME OF THE buildings stayed about five or six stories tall, but more started to soar much higher.

The honking of car horns was starting to get to her, as was the sometimes slow-moving traffic. It wasn't as bad as she'd expected. Not yet.

One block was filled with small restaurants on both sides of the street. "How do you know which places are any good?" she asked. "There are so many. On this block alone, I saw Irish, steaks, sushi, hummus, Mexican, Afghani, a tap house, and Renaissance - whatever that is."

"Most people will eat in their neighborhoods a lot, so they know if this sushi place is any good because they live or work within a few blocks of here. Someone who lives in Central Park East probably isn't going to come to this block for dinner unless they have some special reason to. They'll go somewhere closer to home."

"There's a pizza place." She pointed to one of the storefronts.

"I know."

"Is that where we're going?"

Dean flipped on his left turn blinker then kissed the back of her hand. "Nope. Trust me."

So many things confused her, but she wasn't going to ask about all of them - like how one remembered which streets went which way and why there were far more trees than she expected.

Or why the public parking lot looked like it was putting cars on a Ferris wheel. He turned left again and a block and a half later, pulled into a parking garage under the hotel bearing his name.

One of the valets jumped up to help him out of his car.

"Mr. K, welcome to your hotel."

"Thanks, Ryan." Dean pulled some cash out of his pocket and handed it over. "Can you grab my bag?"

Dean walked around to the other side of the car and held the door for Wendy to get out while the young man pulled a small duffel out of the trunk. Dean left her with Frank and Ryan for a moment while he went into the nearby valet office to change.

The men both tried to be polite, but it still felt awkward as she tried to ignore the smell of gasoline and parking garage. On the street outside, the horns and yelling cab drivers sent her heart racing in a different way than Dean's smile.

He emerged looking much more like he had in Trumanville - blue jeans, a rugby shirt, and a winter coat. A knit cap was pulled low on his head. That, combined with the sunglasses in his hand would make him less noticeable.

"My suit is hanging up. Please see it gets to my office." Dean reached for her hand as Ryan nodded. "Thank you." He smiled at her. "Shall we?"

Wendy grinned. "Let's go." There was a pizza place across the street. Perfect. Close by. No wandering the streets of New York.

He didn't try to dart across, jaywalking, but went to the light.

And crossed the wrong direction.

"The pizza place is right there," she said, pointing.

"You're trusting me, remember?"

"Yeah." She took a deep breath. "I didn't realize your office was in a hotel."

"I have several offices throughout the city. This is just one of them."

They walked past the Gershwin Theater where *Wicked* was playing. She wanted to go in and look at merchandise but wasn't going to ask. They had tickets in a few days. She'd go then.

When they reached Broadway, Ellen's Stardust Diner called to her from across the street, but the line to get in was always insane. Or so her internet searches said.

She wished it weren't so cold she needed gloves. Her hand in Dean's just wasn't the same.

They passed what looked like a plaza with a few sculptures and trees and probably places to sit. Was it public grounds or did it belong to the building on the other side?

The crowds seemed to be increasing, which was an issue when they had to condense down to go under the scaffolding in front of a building.

When they passed a giant candy store, she had a thought and looked up at him. "Are we going to Times Square?"

He grinned down at her. "Yep. It was on your list of places you wanted to see."

As she realized there were even more people in front of them, she tamped down her apprehension to let her excitement bubble over. "Yes. Definitely."

"I will tell you not to buy much down here. Most of what you can get here, you can get somewhere else much cheaper."

"Gotcha." Maybe a key ring or something that wasn't expensive to start with was the way to go. When they reached 47th Street, all of the vehicles had to turn.

"They stopped allowing cars a number of years ago," Dean explained. "This part of Times Square is all foot traffic now."

They walked around Times Square for about half an hour, but didn't stop for food right away.

"It's all so much." She stood in the middle of the paved area and turned in a circle, trying to take it all in. Could she see herself living here, even part time? All of it - the noise, the smells, the sights - threatened to overwhelm her.

The hand squeezing her heart threatened to overwhelm her senses.

"Hey. Look at me."

She looked up at Dean, concern reflected in his eyes. "I'm okay. It's just so much."

"It is," he confirmed. "But this is just one part of the city. You don't have to come here if you don't want to." He took her hand again. "Let's go get that pizza."

She nodded, feeling more secure with that bit of contact between them.

"I'd say we should have waited until it wasn't quite so busy, but short of the middle of the night, right before dawn, I'm not sure when that is."

They walked down one of the connecting streets to a pizza place. There were only four bar stools, and they were all in use.

"Come on." Dean carried his two slices of pizza on a floppy plate. She carried hers. He carried both of their soda bottles. She grabbed a bunch of extra napkins. The pizza was a greasy as she'd expected New York pizza to be. It made her mouth water, but she still wanted to soak some of the grease up.

It only took a minute to get back to Times Square where Frank had saved them a table. Frank and the other driver had been wandering around near them, but staying far enough away it wasn't obvious.

They sat down and Dean watched with a barely concealed smirk as she took her first bite.

Wendy closed her eyes and savored. "This is everything I thought it would be."

"I'm glad."

As they ate, they talked about her flight and what she wanted to do while she was in the city.

It helped her relax, but they weren't crowded by other people, even as the crowd flowed around the seating area.

When they finished, they threw away their trash then Dean took her hand, and they walked back to his hotel.

The car waited for them. This time, Frank drove while Wendy and Dean rode in the back. The route had to be different because of the one-way streets but before long, they were back in front of Dean's building.

The lobby was everything she'd seen in the pictures and more.

She found herself clinging to Dean's hand as he greeted the doorman and the concierge at the desk in the entryway.

Except entryway wasn't nearly a fancy enough word for the marble and glass and everything else.

He introduced her and told them she'd be staying with him and should be assisted in any way she needed.

They seemed genuinely happy to see her. It made her feel a little odd, even though she knew she'd have her own bedroom and at least one of his staff members lived there as well.

Then they were in an elevator being whisked to the top floor. "Wait until you see how fast the WiFi is."

She glanced up to see him trying to hide a smirk.

"Also, I've got your lofts into the beta of the new satellite internet you talked about."

Wendy hugged his arm. "Thank you."

They exited into a common area with several doors, which surprised Wendy.

"You don't have your own private entry from the elevator?"

Dean chuckled. "No. I had lots of options when I decided to upgrade my apartment in the city. I could have gone way more upscale than this one. The Dakota, where John Lennon lived and Yoko Ono still does, had an opening. They're notoriously picky about who they let in, but several people I know who live there said I was a shoo-in. Another one on Central Park South would have been nice, but ultimately, I liked this one best, even though it didn't have the most expensive price tag and isn't actually on the park. You can't even see the parade from here."

He led her into the apartment. She barely had time to take any of it in before he took her up a flight of stairs and out another door.

The frigid air shocked her, though she still had her winter outer layer on. They stood on the rooftop.

"This is why I bought this apartment," he told her.

Up here she could barely hear the noise of the city and when she walked to the eastern side, she could look down at that first, shorter building, but mostly she could see the park and the city beyond.

Dean stood behind her and wrapped his arms around her waist. His breath was warm in her ear. "So, what do you think?"

Wendy twisted her head to look up at him. "I think I could get used to this."

Then he kissed her and she knew she'd found the place she wanted to be.

For the rest of her life.

The other stuff didn't matter.

As long as she was with Dean, everything else was just details.

EPILOGUE

Violet Braverman reached down and tugged on the wooden arm on the side of her chair and flipped the footrest out on her recliner.

With a sigh she settled in and pulled the blanket over her legs.

"Up."

Her Yorkie hopped up and settled in between her legs as she turned on her tablet and started to scroll social media.

Trumanville had been on the upswing for a few weeks, and she no longer knew anyone that was sick. They hadn't had a flu season like that in several years.

Technically, it wasn't over, not yet, but it was mid-March, despite the several inches of snow on the ground. The latest she ever remembered getting snow was mid-May.

Scrolling through her feed, she squinted at a few updates that weren't in her chosen, large font. She hated putting her glasses on.

A photo caught her eye. Wendy Milligan updated her profile picture to one of her with that nice Dean from New York.

They were hugging with Wendy's feet off the ground. The courthouse was in the background with one of her snowman windows - the one on the music store - off to the side.

And they looked happy.

The first comment was from Wendy's little sister. That Milligan hadn't had a serious beau in years. Who could Violet think of that might be good for her?

No.

She'd promised herself no more match making.

Wendy and Dean hadn't really been match making. All she'd done was suggest alternative arrangements when that young man needed a place to stay.

The rest had been up to them.

Violet couldn't stop the grin that crossed her face. Sometimes love just needed a little shove.

Thank you for joining Wendy and Dean in Windows of Love!
Merry Christmas!
Be sure to check out the first chapter of
Dinner with a Prince
in a swipe or two! Book 1 in the Prince of New Sargasso series was so much fun to write, and I hope y'all enjoy it to!
Be sure to join my newsletter to be kept up to date on the latest news and new releases!

DINNER WITH A PRINCE PREVIEW

Dinner with a Prince
Available now!

A s the guy in the auto behind her laid on his horn, Karsen Robertson resisted the urge to respond in kind. It wasn't her fault traffic had nearly come to a complete standstill.

Blame the stupid prince, second in line to the throne of New Sargasso, and his entourage blocking off the roads near the New Hope build site. His protection detail required it.

Like anyone cared enough about the ridiculous royal to want to hurt him.

Kari blew out a breath, her golden-brown hair flying as she did.

That wasn't fair.

By all accounts, Prince Gideon was a very kind man and a worthy potential successor to the throne of New Sargasso - should something happen to his older brother. Charismatic. Magnetic dark eyes partially hidden behind glasses that looked more dashing than dorky. Dark brown hair just begging for someone to mess it up.

The horn blared again, and she realized the car in front of her had moved up several feet. Easing off the brake, she inched forward.

The drive to work, which should have taken maybe fifteen minutes, took nearly forty-five. At least her parking spot was protected, and therefore, still empty.

Kari wrapped her apron around her waist, tying it behind her as she rushed into the bakery.

"You're late." There was no anger or malice in Mama Josie's voice.

"Stupid prince has roads blocked off." She stashed her purse under the counter.

"You've known for a week he'd be there." Mama Josie handed her a cup of coffee, fixed just the way Kari liked it. "Roads are always blocked off for an event like this."

The prince wasn't just stopping by the house being built. He was doing a tour of the whole revitalized area.

He might even stop by the bakery.

Or so Mama Josie believed.

The house was blocks away. There were closer places to stop for a photo opp. No one believed he'd actually have lunch or a snack that wasn't fully vetted first.

Not when he was second in line for the throne of New Sargasso.

"Get to work," Mama Josie reprimanded lightly after Kari took several sips of her coffee. "There might not be many people here because of Prince Gideon, but that doesn't mean we won't have a big rush later."

"Yes, ma'am." Kari snapped a sloppy salute.

Mama Josie shook her head and went back to rolling out her dough.

Kari didn't touch the food before it was baked. She'd tried. It hadn't worked. Even when Mama Josie put it in the oven, gave her strict instructions on when to pull it out, somehow Kari had managed to mangle everything.

Once baked goods were cooled, she was fine. Before that? Forget it.

Mama Josie kept her around anyway because they'd realized how much they needed each other before discovering Kari's lack of skill.

A few of their regulars popped in for coffee and meat or veggie pasties. A few customers she didn't know also stopped in, but overall the morning was slower than normal. Mama Josie still made way too much. She always did. Anything leftover would be given to a senior center located a few blocks away.

The prince was supposed to stop there this morning, too.

"You're looking a bit at odds, dear."

Kari poured more coffee for Mrs. Steinert. "Just running late because of the prince's stupid traffic jam this morning. It's got me discombobulated."

"Maybe he'll come down this way." Mrs. Steinert came in the late morning every day, ate her meat pie, drank her coffee, and tried to set Kari up with one of her several grandsons or any other male within Kari's general age range. That meant any male between eighteen and thirty-eight or so. It didn't matter whether a man was tall or short, full head of hair or completely bald, or even if he had all of his teeth - or any. Mrs. Steinert had, for some reason, decided it was her life's mission to see Kari happily married.

"I wouldn't count on it. I'm quite certain the prince has better things to do with his time than stop by here for a couple of pasties." She took Mrs. Steinert's trash as the woman enjoyed her second cuppa.

"The two of you would have gorgeous children together."

The absurdity of the statement struck Kari, and she couldn't stop the laughter from bubbling up. She finally set the coffee pot down so she wouldn't drop it and make a mess.

Her hands rested on her knees as she laughed until she could barely breathe. Tears rolled down her cheeks as she managed to open her eyes enough to see Mrs. Steinert's amused grin.

"Can't you just see it?" Kari gasped as the bell jangled over the door. "Me and the prince having babies?"

"I don't know." A new voice came from behind Kari. "It's been a while since I had a woman offer to bear my children. It might be worth having a conversation about it."

Prince Gideon of New Sargasso knew the smirk on his face wasn't his best look but also knew women found it irresistible.

Or so the tabloids said.

He'd never tested it.

But he'd never had a woman absolutely laugh at the thought of being the mother of his children before.

The woman, with long golden-brown hair tied back at the nape of her neck, and tear tracks on her cheeks as color flooded them, straightened. Her blue eyes had gone wide with shock.

That reaction wasn't uncommon to his sudden appearance somewhere.

The lack of deference or even a curtsy or head bob was unusual.

"Welcome to Walkabout. Can I get something for you?"

Gideon looked around the bakery. Clearly Australian in nature, some of it - like the giant, but not quite life-sized, stuffed kangaroo - seemed to be a bit overkill.

He was about 90% sure it wasn't a taxidermied animal but rather a nearly life-like fake.

"What do you recommend?" he finally asked, taking note of her name tag. "Whatever you think I might like will be fine, Kari."

Rather than the normal wide-eyed awe at his use of her name, her eyes narrowed. "It's not Care-ee. It's Kah-ree. What if I offer you Stargazy pie or winkles?"

His smirk turned into a full-fledged grin. "Those are both British delicacies. This is an Aussie bakery."

"Witchetty Grubs?"

He winked at her. Not one of his usual moves. "Not really a bakery kind of item, but they're not bad."

She moved behind the counter and poured a cup of coffee - in a to-go cup - and packaged what appeared to be a meat pie. Pushing them toward Gideon, she named a price.

Though normally one of his staff members paid for anything that wasn't given to him, Gideon wanted to take care of this himself. He reached into the inside breast pocket of his sport coat and pulled out his wallet.

"Oh, no!" Another woman came out of the kitchen, her eyes snapping. "This is on us. Karsen Mikayla," she hissed. "Where are your manners?"

She shrugged. "He can afford it."

Gideon tried to suppress a grin, but he wasn't completely successful. He pulled a few bills out, far more than the price Kari quoted, and set them on the counter. "It's my pleasure to pay for my own meal."

"I won't take it," the second woman warned.

"Mama Josie, let the man pay for his food," Kari muttered.

Taking the cup and Styrofoam container, Gideon walked to the table where Kari had been when he walked in. "Would you mind if I joined you?" he asked the woman sitting there.

"Please, have a seat, Your Royal Highness. I'd be happy to have you join me." The woman actually batted her eyelashes at him as he sat down. "I'm Mrs. Steinert. You should ask her out."

Gideon nearly choked on his sip of coffee. "Pardon?"

"Kari. You should ask her out."

This time his sip was more measured, and only when he was certain Mrs. Steinert wasn't talking. "So she can have my children?" Did he manage to keep his face from showing his amusement?

Mrs. Steinert simply raised an eyebrow. "Those children would be quite lovely if they were to look anything like their mother."

He leaned back in his chair, stretching his legs in front of him, purposely projecting a picture of being completely at ease. In reality, he remained acutely aware of the members of his staff purchasing their own food and the members of the media straining to peer through the window.

Gideon let one eyebrow lift as he focused his attention on Mrs. Steinert. "And if they looked anything like their father in this scenario?"

Those eyelashes went to work again as he saw Kari move their direction out of the corner of his eye. "They'd be dashing and heart breakers and far too handsome for their own good."

Kari snorted. "Don't say things like that to him, Mrs. Steinert." She refilled the woman's coffee cup. "His head is far too big already, especially for someone who doesn't do much of anything."

That stung a bit. Yes, Gideon lived a life of privilege and wealth, but he worked and worked hard. That work didn't often include physical labor, but he didn't sit around and eat bon bons or watch stories on the box with his feet up. He'd made over four hundred appearances in the last year alone, many of them to raise funds for one organization or another.

And that didn't include his time in the military.

Instead of letting her know how much it bothered him, he turned on his best smile. "Well, then, Kari, why don't you have dinner with me? Or would you rather turn me down and deflate my ego just a bit?"

Dinner with a Prince
Available now!

He doesn't want to be king.
She doesn't want to be a princess.
He doesn't have a choice.
She does.

Princes of New Sargasso
Book 1

Prince Gideon of New Sargasso is used to people deferring to him.

He's even had supermodels offer to have his babies - quite a sacrifice for someone who makes their living in bikinis.

So when he walks into a local Aussie-inspired café to find Karsen Robertson laughing to the point of tears at the idea, he's a little shocked.

Then she makes him pay for his food.

No one does that.

But nothing and no one has intrigued him quite like the blue-eyed beauty who has nothing but snark for him.

Of course he's going to ask her out.

And, if he can keep the paparazzi and tabloids away long enough, finagle a way to make her a
princess.

But if she's not sure about the princess thing, how would she feel about one day becoming
queen?

First dinner with a prince.

Then a crown.

If she doesn't run screaming first.

LETTER TO READERS

Dear Reader,

Thank you for joining Wendy and Dean in *Windows of Love*! I appreciate you and hope you enjoyed it!

I'm so glad Dean finally got his happy ending! I always hated that he was left to pick up the pieces of his life after Kim went crazy in *Falling for Mr. Write*!

Serenity Landing Book Club

What is that?! It's the Facebook reader group and I'd love to have you there! It's easier for you to see what's posted than on a Facebook page and we do fun stuff! There will be discussion questions after the release of a book, sneak peeks of the next one, general discussion, and chances to win copies of books and other goodies! I'd love to have you there!

Other Stuff

I see a meme floating around Facebook from time to time that tells readers what they can do to help their favorite authors. Buying their next book or giving a copy away is kind of a no-brainer, but the biggest thing you can do is write a review. If you enjoyed *Windows of Love* would you consider doing just that?

I would LOVE to hear from you! My email address is books@carolmoncado.com. To stay up-to-date on releases, you can sign up for my newsletter (there's fun stuff - like a chance to get *Love for the Ages* free! You'll also get notices of sales, including special preorder pricing! And I won't spam!) or there's always my website :). You can find my website and blog at www.carolmoncado.com. I blog about once a month at www.InspyRomance.com. And, of course, there's Facebook and my Facebook page, Carol Moncado Books. But... the way pages work, sometimes very few people (often 1-5% of "likes") will see anything posted. I keep trying to find the best way to get to know y'all and "spend time" together outside of your Kindle - at least for those of you who want to!

Thanks again!

ACKNOWLEDGMENTS

They say writing is a solitary endeavor, and it absolutely can be. Sitting in front of the computer for hours on end, talking to imaginary people.

And having them talk back ;).

But the reality is no one walks alone. Since I began this writing journey many years ago, I can't begin to name all of those who've helped me along the way. My husband, Matt, who has always, *always* believed in me. All of the rest of my family and in-loves who never once looked at me like I was nuts for wanting to be a writer. Jan Christiansen (my "other mother") has always believed in me and Stacy Christiansen Spangler who has been my dearest friend for longer than I can remember.

Ginger Solomon, author of *One Choice* and a bunch of other fantastic books (but *One Choice* is still my favorite!), has been invaluable with her proofreading services. Check her books out!

Then there's my writer friends. Bethany Turner (have you read *The Secret Life of Sarah Hollenbeck* or *Wooing of Cadie McCaffry* yet?! And *Hadley Beckett's Next Dish* is coming soon!) and Mikal Dawn (AH! *Count Me In!*) have both been so wonderful the last few months keeping me laughing and my spirits up. Then Jennifer

Major, a Canadian no less ;), who does life with me and loves me anyway! There's Jen Cvelbar (writing as Jennifer A. Davids and the best case of misidentification *ever*, not to mention best conference roomie - and has a new book coming next summer! YAY!), and Stacey Zink who helped so much recently. There's my MozArks ACFW peeps who laugh with me, critique, and encourage to no end. Then there's all of the others who've helped me along on this journey.

And my first reader crew, which has expanded over the years, are ALL INVALUABLE to my writing process! I have NO IDEA what I'd do without my first readers and brainstormers - Emily N., Tory U., Jennifer M., Linda F., Ginger L. - my fabulous new team of second readers - Vickie O., Julie G., Emily G. - and my AMAZING assistant Becky H.!

I said I could go on for days, and I could keep going. On and on. I know I've forgotten many people and I hate that. But you, dear reader, would quickly get bored.

So THANK YOU to all of those who have helped me along the way. I couldn't have done this without you and you have my eternal gratitude. To those of you who bought or borrowed this little story, you have my eternal gratitude. I hope you stick around for the next one!

And, of course, last but never, *ever*, least, to Jesus Christ, without whom none of this would be possible - or worth it.

ABOUT THE AUTHOR

When she's not writing about her imaginary friends, USA Today Bestselling Author Carol Moncado prefers binge watching pretty much anything to working out. She believes peanut butter M&Ms are the perfect food and Dr. Pepper should come in an IV. When not hanging out with her hubby, four kids, and two dogs who weigh less than most hard cover books, she's probably reading in her Southwest Missouri home.

Summers find her at the local aquatic center with her four fish, er, kids. Fall finds her doing the band mom thing. Winters find her snuggled into a blanket in front of a fire with the dogs. Spring finds her sneezing and recovering from the rest of the year.

She used to teach American Government at a community college, but her indie career, with over thirty titles released, has allowed her to write full time. She's a founding member and former President of MozArks ACFW and is represented by Tamela Hancock Murray of the Steve Laube Agency.

www.carolmoncado.com
books@candidpublications.com

facebook.com/AuthorCarolMoncado

twitter.com/CarolMoncado

amazon.com/author/carolmoncado

bookbub.com/authors/carol-moncado

Princes of New Sargasso
Dinner with a Prince
Masquerade with a Prince
Secrets of a Prince
Redemption of a Prince

The Beaches of Trumanville
Small Town Girls Don't Marry Hollywood Hunks
Small Town Girls Don't Marry Secret Princes
Small Town Girls Don't Marry Their Best Friends
Small Town Girls Don't Marry Baseball Stars
Small Town Girls Don't Marry Their Back-Ups

The Monarchies of Belles Montagnes Series
(Previously titled The Montevaro Monarchy
and The Brides of Belles Montagnes series)
Good Enough for a Princess
Along Came a Prince
More than a Princess
Hand-Me-Down Princess
Winning the Queen's Heart
Protecting the Prince (Novella)
Prince from her Past

Guardian of her Heart (related novella,
Betwixt Two Hearts Crossroads Collection)

Serenity Landing Second Chances
Discovering Home
Glimpsing Hope
Reclaiming Hearts

Crowns & Courtships

8

Heart of a Prince
The Inadvertent Princess
A Royally Beautiful Mess
The Indentured Queen
Her Undercover Prince
The Spare and the Heir
Beyond Titles & Tiaras
The (Elusive) Princess
It's (Royally) Complicated

Crowns & Courtships Novellas
Dare You
A Kaerasti for Clari
Love for the Ages
(available free as a thank you to newsletter subscribers - click here to join)

Serenity Landing Tuesdays of Grace
9/11 Tribute Series
Grace to Save

Serenity Landing Lifeguards
Summer Novellas
The Lifeguard, the New Guy, & Frozen Custard
(previously titled: The Lifeguards, the Swim Team, & Frozen Custard)
The Lifeguard, the Abandoned Heiress, & Frozen Custard

Christmas Novellas
Serenity Landing Teachers
Gifts of Love
Manuscripts & Mistletoe
Premieres & Paparazzi

Teachers of Trumanville

Love on Parade
Windows of Love

The CANDID Romance Series
Finding Mr. Write
Finally Mr. Write
Falling for Mr. Write

Mallard Lake Township

Ballots, Bargains, & the Bakery (novella)

Timeline/Order
Crowns & Courtships and Novellas
(the first three can be read in any order,
but technically this is the timeline)
1. *Love for the Ages*
2. *A Kaerasti for Clari*
3. *Dare You*
4. *Heart of a Prince*
5. *The Inadvertent Princess*
6. *A Royally Beautiful Mess*
7. *The Indentured Queen*
8. *Her Undercover Prince*
9. *The Spare and the Heir*
10. *Beyond Titles & Tiaras*
11. *The (Elusive) Princess*
12. *It's (Royally) Complicated*